NIGHT — _____ MAN

Nighttime, and the shadows stretched from doorway to doorway, between the high white walls of some buildings and the rough red brick of others. He slipped from shadow to shadow, his passing the dry rasping of light feet upon stray gravel. He sought out every alleyway, every crawlspace between buildings, every fire escape, and the geography of every rooftop. He moved quickly, his goal to remain unseen and undetected. He listened for the sounds of people in trouble, for the cries of the innocent, and always he was grateful when the night was quiet.

The time he believed to be on his side was running out, and there was much remaining to be done. . . .

ROBERT DRAKE is an educator, author, editor, and literary agent. With Terry Wolverton, he co-edited the anthology _Indivisible: New Short Fiction by West Coast Lesbian and Gay Writers,_ which was nominated for two Lambda Literary Awards, and the anthologies _His: Brilliant New Fiction by Gay Men_ and _Hers: Brilliant New Fiction by Lesbians._ He is the book review editor for the _Baltimore Alternative,_ teaches writing at St. John's College and American University, and resides in Annapolis, Maryland. Currently he is at work on Book Two of _The Man._

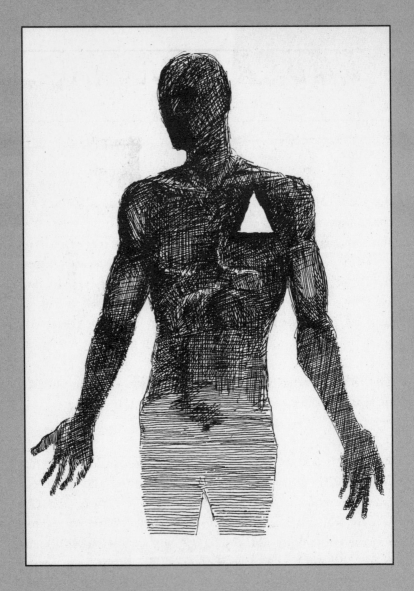

ILLUSTRATIONS BY DERRICK BUISCH

ROBERT DRAKE

THE MAN

A HERO FOR OUR TIME

BOOK ONE: WHY?

A PLUME BOOK

PLUME

Published by the Penguin Group

Penguin Books USA Inc., 375 Hudson Street, New York, New York 10014, U.S.A.
Penguin Books Ltd, 27 Wrights Lane, London W8 5TZ, England
Penguin Books Australia Ltd, Ringwood, Victoria, Australia
Penguin Books Canada Ltd, 10 Alcorn Avenue, Toronto, Ontario, Canada M4V 3B2
Penguin Books (N.Z.) Ltd, 182–190 Wairau Road, Auckland 10, New Zealand

Penguin Books Ltd, Registered Offices:
Harmondsworth, Middlesex, England

First published by Plume, an imprint of Dutton Signet,
a division of Penguin Books USA Inc.

First Printing, June, 1995
1 3 5 7 9 10 8 6 4 2

"Why?" by Somerville, Steinbacher, and Bronski. Used by permission of Jimmy Somerville.

 REGISTERED TRADEMARK—MARCA REGISTRADA

LIBRARY OF CONGRESS CATALOGING-IN-PUBLICATION DATA:
Drake, Robert.
The man : a hero for our time / Robert Drake : illustrations by Derrick Buisch.
p.   cm.
Contents : bk. 1. Why?
ISBN 0-452-27447-8
I. Title.
PS3554.R237M36   1995
813'.54—dc20   94-43614   CIP

Printed in the United States of America
Set in Garamond No. 3, Flash and Tekton

Designed by Steven N. Stathakis

For
George Hallameyer

A masked person is not simply a man or woman whose real identity is hidden, but he is an enigmatic entity standing outside the sphere of ordinary conduct . . . enjoying a freedom of movement and conduct denied to ordinary men. The donning of a mask is believed to change a man's identity and faculties, for the assumed appearance is held to affect the wearer's inner nature and to assimilate it to that of the being represented by the mask.

—*Encyclopaedia of Magic and Superstition*

Contempt in your eyes
As I turn to kiss his lips
Broken I lie
All my feelings denied
Blood on your fist
Can you tell me why?
—SOMERVILLE, STEINBACHER, AND BRONSKI'S "Why?"

THE
MAN

PROLOGUE

"Tell me your secrets."

Twenty-year-old Jesus Alvarez let the taller man press against him in the darkness of this alley. A white slice of light slashed its way past them, echoing into the street, spilling about the parking lot across the way. The tall man and he were shrouded in shadow, hidden from view, standing against a wall behind the dark green bulkiness of a restaurant dumpster. Jesus tilted his neck up to kiss the taller man's lips; the taller man offered them, then pulled them away just short of contact.

"Why should I tell you my secrets?" Jesus mumbled, the words like marbles in his mouth. "I don't even know your name."

The taller man's hands smoothed their way over Jesus' short black hair. "Michael," he said and then, looking down to Jesus, smiling, he said again: "My name is Michael."

Jesus lay his head on Michael's shoulder, pressed his arms about this man, felt the broadness of his back, the soft calm rhythm of his breathing. Jesus pressed his groin against Michael's and pulled his head back from Michael's shoulder to look up to Michael's face, the kind expression there, the gentle watching.

Michael's hands moved from stroking Jesus' hair to run the backs of fingers along the line of Jesus' jaw. Jesus guided the fingers to his mouth, where he kissed them, pressed the knuckles to his lips, murmured low moaning sounds upon them. "My secrets," Jesus said.

"Your secrets," Michael repeated and his fingers moved now about the planes of Jesus' face. His thumbs brushed back along the lines of Jesus' cheekbones and up to roll about just under Jesus' eyes. "Your secrets."

Jesus was thinking of his secrets when Michael's thumbs dug upward sharply, yanking into the space of his eye sockets and pressing outward, Michael feeling the jellylike sacs bend under the pressure of his thumbs then feeling the rip as nerves, muscles, skin gave way.

Jesus screamed and Michael kneed him in the groin to shut him up. When Jesus tried to double up, Michael's right strong-armed him back against the wall and with his left Michael searched but a moment for the piece of lead piping he had left hidden there earlier, on the ground close to the wall, before he had ventured further into the night, toward the music, the noise, the smoke and Jesus.

Michael let Jesus go and stepped back. Jesus crumpled forward and Michael stepped clear, watched him fumble around in the alleyway for a moment. Blood painted Jesus' face red. Michael tapped Jesus under the chin with the end of the lead pipe. "Hey faggot," Michael said, "right here," and he swung the lead pipe so he held it in both hands and he used its length to pull Jesus upright, to press him back against the wall, the pipe hard against the cartilage of Jesus' trachea. For a moment, Michael played, listening to the difference in Jesus' breathing the harder he pressed the pipe against the boy's throat.

"Cocksucker," he said. In one fluid movement, Michael took the pipe away from Jesus' throat and, using his right, shoved the pipe hard into the boy's mouth. Teeth broke. He took it out and shoved it in again. More teeth shattered. Using his height as leverage, the pipe deep in Jesus' throat, he forced the boy down on his knees. He reached his left arm around to hold Jesus solid where he knelt and with a hard twisting shove of the lead pipe drove the metal through the back of Jesus' neck. Michael's left took the bloodied end of the pipe in hand and, in a sharp wrenching movement, he twisted the boy's head off.

Michael shook the lead pipe free. There was around him the silence of the night.

WHY?

CHAPTER
One

*M*atthew was cleaning the apartment. In his faded yellow T-shirt and red cotton shorts, he'd dry-mopped hardwood floors and wet-mopped kitchen linoleum; he'd shaken out throw rugs off the front porch; he'd scrubbed tile and cleaned sinks and toilets and mirrors and bathtubs. Now he was dusting.

The stereo was going gangbusters with the slow, pumping rhythm of Madonna Justifying (Her) Love. Matthew took the dustcloth, ran it over the first bookshelf, ran it between his legs like a stripper with a boa and then tried to make an erotic act of spraying Pledge onto a dirty rag. Saggy white tube socks helped slide him across a few feet of wood over to the other bookcase. He dusted the bookcase. Madonna started to bellow how "Love is understanding" and asking for someone to Rescue (Her).

Matthew twisted his way over to a sideboard covered with

knickknacks. He dusted the sideboard, he dusted the knickknacks, he moved them around, he put them back where they had been.

He sang along, doing a grind reminiscent of a dirty hula while twirling the rag in the air. "R-e-s-c-u-e me." He pumped himself in a circle and faced Adam, standing by a just-closed front door, five grocery bags by his feet and a bemused expression on his face.

Matthew was caught off-guard only for a second, and found himself using the moment to appreciate his pure physical attraction to this man, his partner: six feet tall, well-muscled, Adam Morgan at thirty-two looked better than most men in their twenties, with his smile, the line of his jaw strong but flawed, subtly weakened about the chin. A shock of black hair had fallen across Adam's eyes in his climb up the stairs, his arms filled with groceries, and Matthew watched him now as he reached up and brushed the hair casually back into place. Adam's eyes were brown.

Matthew fell back into his boogie. He bumped his way over to Adam, ground his hips against those of his partner and Adam met him halfway with a kiss. "Affectionate tonight, eh?" Adam drew Matthew close to him, his arms wrapping about Matthew, his hands clasping at the small of Matthew's back. "Practicing for that part-time job you're gonna have to get next time we can't make the rent?"

Matthew pulled back, surprised. "Part-time?"

"Yeah yeah," Adam said. His hands unclasped; he reached up with his right hand and brushed the straight, dark brown bangs—the color of burnt sienna from their childhood Crayola boxes—out of Matthew's happy, bright green eyes. The bangs fell back across Matthew's forehead; the routine of it made Adam smile and he kissed Matthew there. Adam liked the way Matthew's five-foot-ten frame fit against his broader bulk, Matthew's body still schoolboy-wiry at thirty-five, Matthew's head nestling comfortably against Adam's shoulder, the hollow of his throat.

Adam let his hands drift down to grasp, to squeeze Matthew's butt quickly. He pushed Matthew away from him slightly, reached down and picked up two grocery bags, which he handed to Matthew just as Madonna faded away with the thrum-thrum of a heartbeat. "Floor show's over. Let's put this shit away." Adam walked off toward the kitchen.

Matthew followed, settling the bags he carried upon the kitchen floor, at Adam's feet, before pausing to lean in the door-way while Adam settled his grocery bags upon the kitchen coun-tertop. "Teach any great minds today?"

Adam looked into the gaping mouths of the bags, reached in and began selecting cans of food, a package of raisins. "A few, I guess." He shrugged, and turned away to put cans of refried beans in the cupboard. "Business as usual. You?" Matthew left the doorway to hand him a few cans of soup from a bag on the floor. Adam put those away too.

"Okay."

Adam closed the cupboard door, looked over at Matthew and grinned. "Okay?"

Matthew shrugged now. "Okay." He bit absently at a finger-nail. "I got a few pages done."

"Good. That's good."

" 'S okay." Adam handed Matthew an empty paper bag, which Matthew folded. Adam moved around him to open the refrigerator. He took a carton of eggs from a paper sack on the floor and began loading them into the egg bin. Matthew said, "Ophelia called."

"Yeah?" Now Adam's head was buried in the freezer, where he was stacking beef steaks and swordfish, two packages of chicken breasts.

Matthew ran his fingers along the folds of the paper bag. "She wanted to know if we wanted to come over for dinner tonight."

"Tonight?"

"For our anniversary," Matthew set the folded bag aside and crossed his arms over his chest. "Our fourth anniversary. They thought it might save us the expense of dining out. Besides, they haven't seen us in a while and you know how they like to, I don't know, do these kinds of things for people. For friends. For us."

Adam banged his head on the freezer door. "Ouch!" he said and backed away carefully from the refrigerator. The freezer door swung shut. Adam rubbed at the sore spot on his skull. He looked to his partner and started grinning again. "Four years?"

"Four years."

"You're probably wondering where your flowers are."

"Far be it from me to ascribe displays of affection to you."

"Oh yeah?" Adam reached out and pulled Matthew to him. He wrapped his arms about his partner. He kissed him. Matthew kissed back. "How's that for affection?"

"Better, but you're still in deep shit."

Adam kissed him again, deeper this time. "Dearest," he said, "is there anything, anything I could do to make it up to you?"

"Promise you'll spend the rest of our relationship as a bottom?"

"No way."

"Hmm." Matthew pressed his head against Adam's chest, and listened to the soft thumping of his partner's heart. Adam kissed the top of his head. Matthew said, "I've been cleaning all afternoon. I probably stink."

"To high heaven." Adam's hand rumpled Matthew's hair. "Hey, go shower." Adam slapped Matthew on the ass the way jocks do in a ball game after a particularly good play.

Matthew yelped, turned, and headed off down the hallway. Adam looked down at the partially disemboweled bags about his feet. He knelt to gather packages of pasta. From the bathroom, he heard the sounds of running water and Matthew singing the words to "Like a Virgin."

Fruit, Adam thought, grinning. *Four years—kee-rist,* and he put the pasta away, in a cupboard above the counter, next to the place where they kept the spaghetti sauce. He stared at the open cupboard for a moment, at the small space of darkness above the bright colors of the metal cans. He closed the cupboard door and walked slowly toward the living room.

The shower was running. He heard that. Matthew was singing; he heard that too. His fingers reached up and undid the tie hanging about his throat. He pulled at it and opened the top button of his shirt as he walked down the darkened hallway toward the bathroom.

He placed his hand upon the wood of the bathroom door. It opened silently. Light streamed in across peach-colored tiles from a window on the far wall. The glass door of the shower to Adam's immediate right was covered by steam, and behind it, Adam could see the blurred pink form of Matthew's body.

Adam closed the bathroom door behind him, turning the knob as he did so it clicked quietly into place. He slipped past the glass doorway, stood before the sink and toilet and undressed, hands moving over pale, hard plastic shirt buttons, the zipper of a fly; pulling at the elastics of socks and underwear and, finally, the tugging of a T-shirt over his head momentarily blinding him with a wrapping of white. He left the clothes on the floor and moved toward the shower.

The glass door opened and Adam slipped inside, taking Matthew from behind, his arm wrapping about Matthew's chest, moving to scissor a right nipple between fingers, moving to brush across the muscles of Matthew's chest and belly, the hair there plastered down by water, moving lower still to grasp the thickening shaft of flesh, to cup in his hands the balls of his partner.

He prodded Matthew from behind with his cock. "I love you," he said. "Matthew, I love you completely."

Matthew braced himself against the wall; Matthew moaned as Adam bit tenderly at his ear.

Water washed over them.

•   •   •

13

MATTHEW FOLLOWED ADAM down the stairwell of their apartment building, the new carpeting of the steps feeling springy beneath his feet. The collar of Matthew's tweed blazer had gotten turned under when he swung the jacket on; he tugged at it now to try and straighten it out. When they reached the bottom landing, Adam held the door open and snagged Matthew's collar into proper alignment as he passed. Matthew flicked him a grateful grin.

They walked through the courtyard of their building, a dark brick and wood co-op built in the 1920s. They didn't talk much, taking in the feeling of the walk and the balm of the air. Matthew and Adam shared a relaxed, loping kind of gait that moved them quickly yet unhurriedly through crowds, airport terminals, train stations, grocery stores and along sidewalks to friends' apartments.

Twenty minutes later the two men bounded up a step onto a private walk leading to the front door of a converted Victorian row house. They passed gas lamps on either side of the walk, original to the building's construction. Recently repainted black, the lamps held blue and yellow flames that wavered behind bubbled glass in the onset of twilight. A small breeze passed Adam and Matthew as they reached the front door, bringing with it the smell of supper from someone's nearby kitchen: roasted meat and soft spices. The door was open and they pushed in, Matthew leading, Adam following.

They climbed two flights of thinly carpeted stairs to stand before a white painted door. A red street bicycle leaned against a wall; a fire extinguisher hung above it. Adam rang the buzzer. The piece of paper taped above it said "Rodriguez-Stern."

The door swung open to reveal the smiling, dark face of Ophelia Stern. She held a flat spatula aloft in greeting. "Come on in boys," she beamed. "Supper's on!"

Adam and Matthew both smiled at the sight of this familiar, loved woman. "Thanks, Oph'," Adam said, and bent to kiss her cheek as he passed her, into the house, headed for the kitchen and, he knew, Ophelia's lover Elizabeth. Matthew murmured "Hi" and stopped to hug Ophelia. Both men ignored her nouvelle Aunt Jemima dialect; before seizing her position as Channel 7's chief investigative reporter, Ophelia Stern had held vast theatrical ambitions. The actress inside of her bubbled up now and then through her still-active penchant for accents of all types.

A large, pale-colored mongrel came running, nails clattering, feet skidding on the hardwood floors, happy at last to leap up at Matthew, who tore himself from Ophelia's embrace to squat low and let the dog ravage his face with fast, wet kisses. His hands swiftly moved to scratch the dog behind the ears. While dodging the dog's kisses he said, "Yes, yes Bruce, I've missed you too. I have." He drew the dog close to him, hugged the warmth of the animal. "Oh-it's-so-good-to-see-you."

He let go of the dog with a playful swat and stood to see Ophelia smiling at him, her hand still on the handle of the open door. He moved as though to apologize and she shushed him with, "No hurry, girlfriend, no hurry. Door's open, door's shut, you one white boy I know ain't going away." She shut the door behind them, calling out into the apartment, "Elizabeth, company's come callin'!"

Matthew followed her into the house. He smelled the food cooking, the same smells hinted at in the breeze below. He heard the laughter and the sounds of Adam's voice with Elizabeth's as they traded news: quick jabs of wit and love. Entering the kitchen, he saw Elizabeth's smiling face turn toward him and fill with happiness at his presence. He saw this, and he saw Ophelia swat Adam's hand as he tried to steal a fingertipful of mashed sweet potatoes from a pot upon the stove.

"DINNER WAS GREAT." Matthew let out a belch that rumbled about the Victorian cornices of the buildings they passed while he and Adam walked home from Ophelia and Elizabeth's, a slight distance at fifteen blocks. The air was filled for a moment with the smell of garlic, tomatoes, steak, butter and, slightly, coffee.

Adam wrinkled his nose as the smells curled about him. "Phew," he said, and waved his hand in front of his face. "You get home, you brush your teeth or I know one faggot in this city who won't be getting laid tonight."

"I'm sure you know more than one, dear," Matthew said. The coffee had wound them both up a little bit; the walk back would calm them down. Matthew reached out and snared Adam's hand in his.

The sound was brittle about them at first, like the falling tinkling of broken glass. It was laughter, and it poured from the shadows of the buildings around them, growing louder, and closer, bringing with it the sharpness of the silence beneath it, the absence of all other sounds, the absence of all other people, of car tires rolling along asphalt.

He stepped out of the shadows of an alleyway, a teenager in a denim jacket. He was of average height with average looks. A metal baseball bat draped across his shoulders like the beam of a crucifix, his wrists over either end to keep the bat in place. Two other youths—one taller, one shorter; one stouter, one thinner— followed him from the darkness, carrying with them similar gleaming shafts of aluminum.

Adam and Matthew let their hands fall to their sides, their memory filling with Ophelia's recent Channel 7 News stories on the increase of violent hate crimes reported in the City. Beyond the shoulders of the three youths they could see, a block away, the well-lit safety of Washington Street, a major thoroughfare thick with gleaming streetlamps and passing traffic.

"Aw shucks, boys," the young kid said, "there's no need for you to stop holding hands 'cause we're here."

Adam's fists clenched and unclenched. Everything seemed preternaturally bright to him, clear and vivid.

"Is there, fellas?"

Matthew cleared his throat and stepped forward half a step, reaching toward his back pocket. "Look, if it's money you w——"

The thickset lout behind the kid spoke: " 'Tain't money."

Matthew spoke again. "What, then?"

There was silence. Silence in which Adam and Matthew could contemplate how best to reach the safety of Washington Street. Silence in which the three youths could take up their baseball bats and begin pounding them softly against the flesh of their palms.

Adam and Matthew turned and ran. They ran back into the shadows of the buildings, of the alleys that ran behind them, away from streetlamps and passing car headlights, toward dumpsters, garbage cans and the bloated dark corpses of stuffed trash bags. They didn't listen to hear if the youths were following them, they didn't think about where they were running to, they only ran; a thick, blinding run on legs fueled by fear and driven by instinct.

They reached the dead end of an alleyway lined with trash cans and they collapsed, Matthew sagging back against the brick wall of an old building, Adam falling to his knees on ancient cobblestone.

Matthew let his head roll back upon his shoulders and he prayed, quickly. He shut his eyes. He opened them. The sky was black. No stars. His head fell forward and he saw, a hundred feet away or less, the passing dark bodies of cars, the quiet roaring of their rolling tires upon the asphalt and he saw the edges of the light, the pools of light beyond this alley, beyond this private world.

He heard the roaring of his own breathing in his ears.

It was Washington Street.

Matthew reached down to tap Adam on the shoulder and when Adam looked up, Matthew pointed toward the street. Adam nodded. The youths were gone. Matthew stepped away from the brick wall.

Matthew's head hammered forward, caught by the speeding swing of the lead pipe at the base of his skull, lurching him onto Adam and knocking him sideways to the ground, upon his back. Matthew was yanked up, off Adam, and Adam could see a tall, sturdily built form in a long coat holding Matthew up with one hand. The tall man—not a boy, like the three youths earlier, but a man—threw Matthew up against the wall, his body clattering against the tin lids of hollow trash cans. In his other hand the tall man held a thick piece of lead pipe and he used it now to whack Matthew hard from right to left across the face. Adam thought he heard the crack, the breaking of a bone and he was up, he was standing and there was a flash of pain in his ankle and he fell, he went down again and there was a yanking he was up and a heavy hand threw him up against the other wall of the alley and he ducked and the lead pipe whooshed by above his head.

Adam lunged forward and tackled the tall man. He grabbed him about the waist and used his body weight to bring him down to the ground. In the background, far, it seemed away from them, he heard something that sounded like Matthew groaning.

The lead pipe clipped Adam under the chin and sent him flying back, off of the tall man, who now rose, steadily, to his feet. Adam crouched there, in the alley, his breath coming in ragged small gulps. He tasted blood in his mouth; a small trickle of it had slipped from the left corner of his mouth and he licked at it. The tall man stood before him now, strong, confident, the lead pipe hanging loosely in his right hand, at his side.

The tall man smiled, tightly at first, then broadly. He turned and stepped toward Matthew, twisted still upon the trash cans.

No.

Adam stood.

No.

God.

The tall man stroked Matthew's hair with his left hand, absently; ran his hand along the leather sleeve of Matthew's jacket. He took the edge of the pipe and played it along the line of Matthew's jaw, Matthew's mouth, Matthew's nose, his eyes, his brow.

Adam let out a yell and hurled himself on the tall man, knocking him again to the ground and the tall man lost his grip on the lead pipe; Adam heard it clatter to the ground. Adam spun, he moved as the tall man fell and he sat astride the tall man and he used his weight to hold him down he used his knees to pin the tall man's arms to the ground, and he used his fist to punch the tall man in the face. He drew back and clenched his hands together and in two quick motions, hammered the tall man's face, right-left, left-right. "Motherfuck," Adam said and the tall man looked up at him and Adam looked down at the tall man and the tall man had eyes of skylight blue and hair of sandy blond and Adam had eyes of brown and hair of black and the tall man got a small smile across his face and he reared up, he used his elbows and his spine to buck Adam from him like a thirteen-year-old first-time rider at the rodeo. Adam was down on the ground and the tall man kicked him, hard, between the legs with what felt to be a heavy boot. Adam groaned and curled in pain. The tall man stared down at him for a moment, blinked once and, smiling again, moved over to the trash cans where Matthew lay.

The tall man picked up the lead pipe from where it had fallen in the alley and he used it now to draw Matthew upright, pressing the pipe against his throat, against Matthew's windpipe and listening, as he loved to do, to the changes in life-giving breath as he pressed down, let go upon the cartilage. He thrust the end of the lead pipe into Matthew's midsection and Matthew doubled over, only to have the same end of lead pipe catch him on the chin and smack him back upwards once again. He sagged against the brickwork. The tall man stepped back for a moment and contemplated his options.

"No," Adam said. "Please."

Adam tried to rise. The tall man turned to look at him; his face was blank of all expression. Adam said it again: "No. Please."

Then Adam heard the tattooing begin. The lead pipe slammed against ribs, against arms, against the bones of Matthew's face, against legs, against his knees, into his groin. Matthew was pitched about and the pipe was brought down heavily upon his skull, his shoulder blades, the back of his ribcage, across his spine. It slammed into his hips, against his legs, his elbows, his hands. Matthew sagged chest-first against the wall. A dark blood seeped out his mouth.

The tall man walked toward Adam. The tall man slipped the piece of lead piping into a deep front pocket of his coat. He looked down upon Adam, crawling there, trying to rise. He reached down, he grabbed Adam by his shirt collar and yanked him to his feet. He let go, he reached back, he pulled back and he hit Adam square in the face with the thick meaty fist of his right hand. Adam staggered back toward the street and the tall man followed, pulled him upright and hit him again in the face with the broad flatness of his left fist. Adam staggered back again and the man hit him again, kept hitting him, pushing him back toward the street. Adam felt the breaking, the give of shattered cartilage in his nose. A blow to his side gave him the feeling of cracking ribs and the sharp stab of hurt upon breathing.

The tall man started hitting Adam as Adam had hit him, thick fists clenched into one and the blows hammering right-left, left-right, driving Adam back. Whenever Adam started to fall the tall man dragged him upright once more and hit him again, fast, hard, before Adam had a chance to crumple and then they stood there, at the entranceway of the alley, close to the world of pools of light and others. The tall man stepped back and Adam stood there, bloodied, battered and weaving and the tall man shifted a bit and jumped and kicked and Adam went flying out from the edge of the alleyway into the path of a car moving down the street. There was a thump, and the squealing of brakes and cries of "Ohmigod!" and the tall man fell back into the shadows, back toward his lead pipe, back toward the trash cans, and Matthew.

He smiled, and his ears were deaf to the noise, the covering distraction less than one hundred feet away.

LIGHT, BRIGHT WHITE and hurting. His eyes opened, then shut, then opened again. Everything was blurry. A dark form leaned over him. He saw movement above him; he felt the placing of a warm hand upon his forehead. More movement, then the voice, thick and familiar. " 'Lizbeth! He's awake!"

He slept.

CHAPTER
Two

*F*irst there was the cold air pushing itself into his lungs, then the steady thump-thump of his feet upon the pavement, playing counterpoint to the beating of his heart as he ran south from house to harbor, around and back again.

He'd come to like his morning run. It gave him a chance to clear his head, not only from the cobwebs of sleep but also from the fog of life that wrapped itself around him as he tried to slip from day to day.

He was at the harbor now and he turned east to trot along the water's edge, heading toward the oldest part of town. He ran past shiny hotels and shopping galleries, but before him he could see the quiet early-morning thoughtfulness of ancient brick row houses and warehouses, just beginning to warm in the first glimmer of sun.

He bounced on the balls of his feet, keeping the motion going as he waited for the light to change and the traffic to stop. It did and he was off again, across the last major street separating the new city from old town.

Old town. Even the smells changed here, and life wallowed in a permanence it only sat atop in the newer portions of the City.

Life.

Death.

Adam ran on, toward a large brick building on the corner of two old two-lane streets whose cracked pavements showed through to brick beneath. A large yellow sign, paint blistered and peeling but still readable, hung above the weathered green of the building's front door and the door was open; the sour smell of sweat and the tang of liniment washed over Adam as he came to a stop before the building. His legs, his muscles, his skin tingled a little bit; they had ever since the incident, over seven months ago. His breathing fell into place from the run. He stepped inside.

The room was bright with morning light. Sunshine streamed in white through milky panes of frosted wired glass along the top of this large room: frosted glass giving way to brick painted yellow, years ago. The light drifted down thirty feet past the peeling ruins of posters, red posters with black ink, green posters with black ink, yellow posters with black ink, boasting names of young men long ago forgotten.

The floor was wood.

Adam stood in the doorway, baggy grey sweat pants covering his legs, dark in places where sweat had poured from his run. The purple sweatshirt he wore was similarly darkened, under his arms and across his chest, down his back. Once-white athletic socks had fallen to bunch about his ankles; his Reeboks were a mess. He had sprinted today, most of it, most of the way here.

He bent one leg up behind him, stretched it, then did the same with the other. It felt good. Adam had passed this place often on his morning runs, even on the occasional warm evening stroll with Matthew. But he had never been inside. The blistered sign outside read: "Day's Gymnasium: Training Fine Pugilists Since 1938."

Pugilists.

Boxers.

Fighters. Adam sniffed a small sniff of pacifist distaste.

Adam moved away from the doorway, feeling the impact of his rubber-soled sneakers against the polished floor. He walked slowly along the periphery of the room, trying not to get in the way of those at work here. He passed a white boy stretching on a bench, his body dry and fresh; he passed a series of young men, all with sweat curling the hairs about their brows and all standing before punching bags that they pummeled, switching left, right, left, right faster, faster, faster and break, switch. He passed a doorway, through which the sounds and bravado of a locker room could be heard. He walked nearer to the ring.

The black kid in the ring was sharp and fast and moved quickly about the tarp; his Asian opponent, thicker, not quite so wiry, countered him, paced him, guarded his moves and checked him now and again when the kid would get too confident.

Adam watched them parry for a moment.

Adam looked down at the mat.

"Y'wanna learn how ta fight?" Adam jumped a little at the voice behind his right shoulder and turned to face a reddened, tough-skinned old gym rat. "When yer fightin' there's only one thing y'really gotta remember," the old man said, chewing on the stub of a dead cigar as he spoke. He switched it over now without using his hands, his thick, flat tongue pushing the rolled tobacco from the right side of his mouth to the left. "Y'fight from here"—he tapped his head—"and here"—he punched his fist lightly against the flab of his own stomach. Now he shook his head slowly from side to side, reminding Adam of a bulldog. "Y'don't fight from here," and he reached out to tap the place over Adam's heart.

Adam nodded.

Fight.

Defend yourself. Defend loved ones.

Moments later, Adam stood again before the barrel-chested old man, Adam's body still clad in jogging sweats and now, heavy on his hands, boxing gloves. He moved his fingers around inside the inner space of the glove. When he actually went to fight, his fingers would be taped; for now, they were free. The rough leather felt smooth to his touch.

Odd, for him, this finally being here, inside a door he had run past often enough since he took up running as a way to build back the strength his legs had lost from the wheelchair—"Day's Gymnasium: Training Fine Pugilists Since 1938." It wasn't the gym that bothered him; he had been going to gyms for the past several years, ever since close about his thirtieth birthday, when he had wanted to soldier up whatever body he had left, keeping it in shape against the years marching against it. He had worked out, lifting weights, riding Lifecycles and trapping himself in cages of Nautilus-steel devices designed to work this muscle and that. He did it; he liked it. He liked the feeling of his body responding to his demands, he liked the feeling at the end of the workout: muscles stretched out, his body ready, whole and full. He liked the way Matthew got excited over his body, the way Matthew liked moving his hands down the muscles of Adam's chest, across the broad expanse of Adam's back, cupping Adam's buttocks in his hands, rubbing gently the sturdy muscles of his thighs, calves, and arms.

But this was different. Moments earlier, Adam had stood before the squat Mr. Day and said the words "Yes, yes, I want to learn how to fight." Adam had been careful not to wrinkle his nose against the now nearly overwhelming strong sour smell of sweat here, the almost sweet hardness of liniment clearer still in the air. The scents were thick and heavy, growing riper and more pungent as the morning wore on. Mr. Day had laughed at Adam's question: "Fight or box?"

"Fight."

Day had shaken his head then for a second time. He had looked up, still laughing, and was about to speak when Adam, unsmiling and tall, a new resolve strengthening inside of him said: "If you don't teach me, I'll find someone else who will."

Day's smile became a scowl. "They won't be as good."

Adam had shrugged. "Maybe."

"Maybe." Day had snorted, taking the cigar from his mouth and pressing two fingers against a reddened nostril. He blew a wad of greenish snot onto the ground near Adam's feet. Adam held his ground, kept his eyes where Day's eyes would be if he looked back up. He did. "You ever been in a fight, kid?"

Adam had shrugged again, admitting only to: "Grade school."

"Grade school." Again, the ponderous head had wagged; again Day had looked away from him. "Grade school." There had been a moment of silence before Day locked eyes again with Adam and this time Adam noticed something different, something lighter and electric about the old man's blue eyes. "What makes you wanna box now?"

"Fight," Adam had said. "Fight. And, it's . . . personal." A memory of Matthew as he looked lying unconscious in the hospital flashed into Adam's skull, and Adam kicked it away.

"Personal. Personal." Then had come a repeat of Day's earlier lecture of fighting from the head and the gut, not the heart.

Now Day said, "Okay, kid. I'll teach ya." He gestured down toward Adam's gloved hands. "Get 'em wrapped. Put the gloves back on. I'll get someone to spar with ya, see how you are right now. We'll go from there."

"I don't have much time."

Day nodded, those eyes sizing Adam up again. "Who does?" he spat, then Day was off, tromping back across the gym, moving at a slow, ponderous but determined gait, and calling "Hey! Sanchez! C'mere fer a minute, will ya?" Adam watched the thin, darkly handsome Latino kid in grey sweat pants and sneakers loping his way across the floor mat toward Day. The kid had been taking quick turns at the small punching bag, then the larger one behind him to his right. He was fast. He could probably fight hard when he had to. Adam trusted Day to have professional reasons for setting Adam up against Sanchez. The boy shot Adam brief glances as Day talked with him.

Adam taped his fingers. He bent them. They felt stiff but secure in the bandage. Beneath the wrapping still there was the buzzing of his flesh, bone and muscle, the tingling like sleep setting in. He looked up: Day and Sanchez were still talking. Adam picked up his gloves.

". . . kick his ass, all right," Day muttered to Sanchez. "I don't need no faggot yuppies runnin' 'round here, I don't care how much money they got. I got enough not to need someone around who ain't serious."

Adam tapped Day on the shoulder. Day turned around, the grimace on his face easing into a supercilious smile as Adam held out his gloves to be put on, laced up. Sanchez had scurried off, but returned with his hands taped and his gloves ready for wearing. Day readied him as he had Adam.

"Nice and easy, boys," Day said, and he patted Sanchez on the butt twice as the boy turned, walking over to, climbing into the ring on the far side of the gym. Adam watched how Sanchez did it, to be sure when it came his turn. Behind the ropes of the ring, Sanchez stared blankly toward Adam, the youth's right hand moving in a quick, nearly thoughtless ritual to cross himself.

Day put his hand on Adam's shoulder and they started walking toward the ring. "Now, fighting, like boxing, is an art form. Here at Day's Gymnasium, where I've been training fine pugilists since 1938, we take pride in fighting good, clean fights. Our boxers fight fair, fight well, fight with honor. . . ."

Adam tuned him out. Before him was the ring. He looked at Sanchez, looking at him. The boy was wiry, intense. Sweat shined in small lines down the front of his bony chest, along Sanchez's sides, tracing the lines of his ribcage. His sweat pants hung loose on him, and Adam didn't think about what was beneath them except to note that Sanchez had a cute butt; Adam had noticed that when Day had patted the boy's rear. If Adam wasn't married, Adam might've liked to pat the boy's butt too.

". . . and have a good fight!" Day was grinning. He reached out and held up the rope for Adam to enter the ring. Adam entered. "Center ring, boys!"

Adam and Sanchez moved to the center of the ring. Adam wondered if Day really knew Adam was gay or was calling him "faggot" in the general, uneducated, high-school-bully kind of sense. Adam figured the latter and pushed the thought away. Sanchez had nice brown eyes. His body was oddly exciting. Adam pushed those thoughts away as well. He and Sanchez bumped gloves and moved off to their respective corners. As he turned, Adam noticed a thin scar just along the lower left rib line on Sanchez's chest. It was a little paler than the rest of his skin, raised, and smooth, like a delicate garden worm that never saw the sun.

Day hit the round bell on the side of the ring with a small steel hammer and Sanchez began his move toward the center of the ring. Adam copied. The two men moved lightly around in soft circles, bouncing smally on the balls of their feet and getting a gauge of the other's probable speed, stamina, weak points.

Sanchez struck first, a right, aimed at Adam's gut and Adam stepped away, feinted, pushed it back.

Then the punches began coming in faster, and Adam found himself concentrating. It was difficult: so many actions, their separate reactions, choosing the right possibilities from hundreds—Adam felt lost and tried as best he could to keep clear, untouched. A solid blow from Sanchez caught Adam square in his breadbasket and the breath rushed out of him and he staggered back three steps. No good, he thought, no good. *This kind of reacting will get me killed* and then Sanchez threw a right toward Adam's chin and Adam's left went up to block it even as Adam's right lurched out to land in the soft hardness of Sanchez's stomach. Sanchez hadn't been expecting that, Adam knew, and grinned inside his skull. He had done it, he had landed a punch. And then Adam knew that Day was partly wrong: you don't fight using your head, you fight using your instinct, then hope some commonsense smarts will kick in as needed.

Adam became more aggressive. There was the crisp feeling inside his body of adrenaline finding its purpose and in his mind, a startling clarity. A small press of men had gathered about the ring, some of them yelling for Sanchez, a few of them shouting for the "new guy." Adam knew they were there but he tuned them out. Adam focused only on landing punch after punch against the smooth flesh of Sanchez, and the hard muscle and bone of his body.

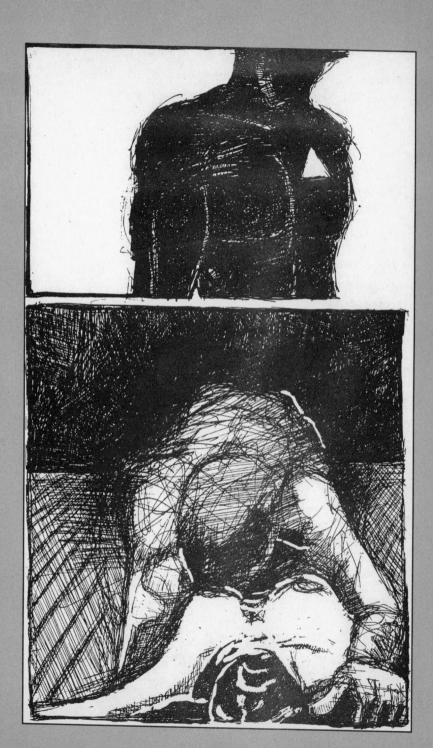

CHAPTER
Three

Skin. The feeling of skin being shrouded in darkness, the feeling of tight cloth wrapping itself across muscles, the feeling of fingers slipping into sheaths of leather gloves.

He looked at himself in the mirror. He wore black from head to foot. He wriggled toes in boots, enjoyed the play of stretching, broadening, flaring the muscles of his shoulders, a feeling like the stretching out of wings beneath the dark fabric of his clothing.

He held it in his hands, he held it out before him. He looked at the sunken emptiness, then hoisted it aloft to draw, to tug it down over his face, erasing the humanity of nose and mouth in a black canvas of night and shadow.

He looked at himself in the mirror. Behind the mask, he blinked his eyes once, twice.

• • •

HE BENT DOWN and took her nipple in his mouth, biting it gently, tenderly, then rougher, feeling it form into a hard little bump between his teeth, feeling the smaller bumps around it rising up to brush his lips. She moaned. "Jimmy," she said.

Her nipple slipped free of his mouth and Jimmy moved his way up her body, tongue licking here, licking there, along the side of her neck. He lay atop her. He looked at her. She looked at him. She smiled. She reached her fingers around the back of his skull to play with a small strand of pale brown hair at the base of his neck. He lowered himself to kiss her; she could feel him, hard, through her skirt, through the denim of his bluejeans. He rubbed himself along her thighs; she tightened her muscles there and he groaned. "Allison," he said, and began kissing the side of her neck, his head buried in her shoulder, his right hand moving up to cup her breast; his rubbing against her leg faster now, insistent and demanding. She let her head roll back upon the pillows of the couch. "Jimmy," she said again, and her eyes closed; her tongue flicked out to wet her lips. She felt a fumbling; Jimmy's hands tugging, grasping, pulling.

He was inside her in a moment and she gasped, started to rise, but he pushed her down. "Allison, Allison," Jimmy mumbled, his face still buried in her shoulder. "Allison." She bit her lip and let go. She could feel him moving inside her, solid, blunt, and thick. She stared up at the ceiling of their trailer. There were holes in the pegboard. She started to count them, but lost place whenever she blinked. In the background she could hear the beating drone of the cheap ceiling fan above the dining table, and the quiet throbbing of the radio playing a tune she couldn't quite make out over the rasping noise of Jimmy's breathing in her ear. His breaths were shorter now, rougher, almost ragged, and his pounding inside her had become something desperate. She knew she should be trying to rise toward this with him, but she felt heavy, weighted down; there was so much water between here and there, and it seemed as though she'd forgotten how to swim. All she could do was lie there, staring through blue, wet eyes toward a light that seemed too far away but that Jimmy reached and, with a yelp, shot into and was through.

He lay atop her still, his weight pressing down upon her, the dampness of shared sweat sticking them together. She could hear his breathing calm, she could hear him swallow, feel the rising and falling gulp of his throat, his Adam's apple against the bone of her shoulder.

She waited. The air was heavy with the bitter smell of rancid, finished sex.

"I'm going out," he said, and rolled off her. Without looking at her he sat on the edge of the couch and tucked himself back into his jeans. Her eyes closed.

He left the sofa and she could hear him walking about behind her. There was the opening of a cupboard door, the sound of a glass being removed, the pouring of the water from the tap, the silence, the sound of his drinking. There was the sound of the glass being set down into the sink.

He gathered his keys and some change and stuffed them back into his front pocket. He jammed his wallet into a back right pocket and picked up his jean jacket from the back of the chair. He swung into it while walking around to the front of the sofa.

He looked at her while he buttoned up the first few buttons from the bottom. He shrugged his shoulders to let the jacket settle on him. She opened her eyes. He stuffed his hands into jacket pockets.

"I'm going out," he said again. She blinked at him once, twice. He turned, walked toward the door, opened it, turned back. "Don't wait up," he said. She blinked at him again and he left, shutting the door behind him.

She shut her eyes and dreamt of sleep.

•　　•　　•

"GET INTO THE GROOVE."

Zach let the music take him away. He swung his arms out, back in, moved his legs, his feet up and down, back and forth to the sounds pounding out of the nightclub's speakers hanging above the rectangular dance floor, to either side and at the center of the dance floor. Thick, bass vibrations rumbled from other, grounded speaker boxes, one to each corner of the dance floor. Zach looked up, toward the ceiling and the array of lights flashing back and forth, computerized circles of color swarming this way and that, combining then separating in a dizzying display of red, white, orange, pink, blue. He closed his eyes and let his neck relax, his head lower and when he opened his eyes he smiled at the man he was dancing with. Dark hair tossing about on the man's head, smooth chest, a T-shirt dampening with sweat the harder the man danced and well-worn 501s hinting at well-defined possibilities. As if reading Zach's thoughts, the man grinned and turned around in his dance. Zach found his mind filling with thoughts of grabbing the man's ass, running his hand over the tight globes of muscle he saw there, his finger along the crack of the man's ass, the man's faded 501s long since shucked off and both of them naked, writhing about on the white sheeting of Zach's bed. The man turned around again in his dance and Zach reached out and pulled him nearer. Zach's arm moving to wrap itself about the other man, drawing him closer; the muscles of their chests pressed together and Zach could feel himself getting hard, and the growing hardness of the other man as well.

They kissed, and Zach tasted the sweet taste of gin and tonic. Zach's other hand reached up to hold the man's head, to run fingers through the thick blackness of the man's hair. The man's hands reached down to cup Zach's ass, to grab it, use it to pull them closer together. The two men separated for a moment, moving to a corner of the dance floor where the man leaned Zach up against the side of one of those booming speakers; Zach felt the bass vibrations rumble through his body, his crotch. The man moved his hands to slip under Zach's T-shirt, to feel the muscles, the velvet darkness of the skin covering Zach's body. His thumbs rolled over Zach's nipples and Zach shivered. They kissed again.

Zach mouthed the words "Let's go" clearly to the other man, who nodded, smiling. They moved to leave the dance floor, the dark-haired man leading, his hand clasped firmly about Zach's hand and keeping them from getting separated in the ever-increasing thickness of the crowd of revelers. There was a period of time, it seemed, in bars such as this one, a period of time between eleven-thirty and one, when the bodies packing into the nightclub increased exponentially. Zach managed a glance at his watch; it was midnight.

Zach and the man pushed their way free of the throng, stumbling toward a door which they pushed open before falling through, out and into the street, the sidewalk, pools of light from streetlamps and the roar of traffic, even at this hour, washing by them. The two men shivered in the wake of a small night breeze, and the dark-haired man crossed his arms over his chest, rubbing his upper arms as if to give them warmth. He grinned to Zach. "So," he said, "your flat or mine?"

Zach grinned back; the man had an accent Zach hadn't been able to pick up in the bar. It was subtle, but it was there and it sounded, to Zach's ear, English. Zach remembered the man's question, remembered visions of twisting bodies on white bedding. "Mine?" The Englishman nodded. "My car's just over here," Zach finished, pointing down the sidewalk toward a darkened patch of parking lot. They started walking off in that direction; they were but a few steps away from the parking lot when Zach reached out and grabbed the dark-haired man by the arm, bringing him to a halt. "I'm sorry," Zach said as the man turned to look at him, "this is really awkward and stupid but I've—" he took a deep breath, let it go; he looked away, he looked back—"forgotten your name."

The other man laughed. "Don't worry about it." He grinned at Zach. "It's Darrin," he said. "Darrin."

"Darrin," Zach repeated. "Darrin." He smiled, reached out, pulled Darrin closer to him. "Darrin," he said, the two men's arms moving to wrap about each other, "how 'bout a little kiss?"

"How 'bout it," Darrin replied, his mouth moving closer to Zach's. They kissed, and Darrin tasted the almost chocolate flavor of rum and Coke and both men heard the rough voice that said:

"Well, well—look what we have here."

NIGHTTIME AND THE SHADOWS stretched from doorway to doorway, between the high white walls of some buildings and the rough red brick of others. He slipped from shadow to shadow, his passing the dry rasping of light feet upon stray gravel. He sought out every alleyway, every crawlspace between buildings, every fire escape and the geography of every rooftop. He moved quickly, his goal the goal of remaining unseen and undetected. He listened for the sounds of people in trouble, for the cries of the innocent and always, he was grateful when the night was quiet.

The time he believed to be on his side was running out and there was much remaining to be done.

"TELL ME WHY?"

Darrin and Zach could still hear the music of the nightclub behind them as they broke away from their kiss to take in the sight of three youths, one to any side of them, the locked abandonment of a closed building behind. The youths held baseball bats, not the wooden kind but the shiny, hard cold silver of aluminum. They pounded the bats gently into the palms of their hands, or swung them around in circles before their waists, or held them casually across one shoulder, as if waiting for a turn at bat. The three youths were grinning at the two men. Zach and Darrin let go of each other completely, moving instinctively to stand a few steps apart.

"Look," Zach began, "if it's money you want—"

The youth standing directly before them, five-ten, sturdily built, pale brown hair, faded bluejeans over powerful legs, denim jacket over a T-shirt stretched tight across his chest threw back his head and laughed at this. "Money? Naw." He tapped the rounded end of the baseball bat a few times on the cement of the sidewalk before him, producing a dull, weighted metal sound. "You fuckers, you cocksuckers always think we want your money." His eyes flicked to either side of the two men, to the other waiting youths. "Is it money we want, boys?"

"Nope," said the one to Zach's left. Lanky at about six foot two and pimpled, with long, thin black hair under a dirty baseball cap, this boy had his bat slung across his right shoulder; his hands worked the grip.

"Ain't money," the last one said, rubbing the bat as if scratching an itch along the inside muscle of his left calf. The shortest of the three, at about five-five, he was also the stockiest, with layers of muscle already turning to fat beneath the yellow sweatshirt and worn brown corduroys covering his body.

The youth standing before them spoke again, the baseball bat now held firm in his hands before him. "We just wanna make the world a better place to be"—his smile vanished—"for decent people." The baseball bat swung out quickly and directed Zach and Darrin toward a darkened area of the parking lot, blocked off from view by the bulky metal presence of two dumpsters and a stacking of old, worn tires. "Move!" the boy yelled, and the other youths closed in, driving Zach and Darrin into the shadows.

There was silence in the shadows. Darrin and Zach were shepherded through the parking lot until they stood trapped, a foot away from a high brick wall. The two men turned around. Ahead of them, in front of two dumpsters and several rows of worn tires stood the three youths, their hands working the grips of their baseball bats. The youth with the pale brown hair, the one in the denim jacket who had spoken earlier, moved in closer toward the two men. He could hear their breathing coming in quickly, and he liked that; it meant fear. *Fucking queer pussies.* His right hand moved to stroke the metal body of the baseball bat; his own breathing began to take on a coarser movement. He felt the fear of the two men filling him, the scent of it washing over him. He flared his nostrils. He grinned without showing teeth. He reached out with the bat and tapped Darrin gently on the chin with its hard metal end. He moved the bat so its tip traced its way down Zach's chest and belly. "I'd say 'Let this be a lesson to you,' but I guess I should say 'Let this be a lesson to others like you,' since you won't live to learn from your—" the baseball bat moved down to nudge Zach in the crotch "—mistake." The boy drew the baseball bat back, falling into the preparatory stance of a league batter at home plate. Both hands on the grip, he drew the baseball bat back over his right shoulder. The aluminum glinted in dim moonlight. The youth looked at the two men. He waited.

"Get 'im, Jimmy," said the lanky boy in the baseball cap.

"Faggots," Jimmy said. He swung.

There was an explosion, a brief flash of light, and an engulfing wave of smoke carrying the dry, chemical smell of flash powder. Jimmy felt the bat hit against something solid, then twist sharply to the left, wrenching out of his hands. The air beside his right ear, the air beside his left ear was cut with the sound of something flying through it. There were the clattering sounds of metal against asphalt; there were the thudding sounds of falling bodies; there was a voice from behind him that Jimmy spun about to face:

"Don't fuck with me, fellas," the voice roared. "This isn't my first time at the rodeo!" In the clearing of the smoke, standing in the shadows between the metal bodies of the two dumpsters, stood a masked man, six feet tall, dressed in a black body suit. A small pink triangle emblem sat above his heart.

Jimmy looked down. The bodies of his friends lay before

him and, again, he heard The Man speak: "Looks like it's just you and me, kid." Jimmy lunged for a baseball bat at the side of one of his fallen buddies. The Man reached down and grabbed the youth in mid-dive by the back of his jacket, halting Jimmy's lunge and lifting him off the ground. "No weapons," he said. "That's not playing fair." He let Jimmy drop, and The Man's gloved fist swung out to connect with the youth's jaw; left, then right, and The Man sent home a solid right to the youth's bread-basket. Jimmy went down, clutching his gut and rolling on the hard tar. The Man bent down low over the youth, a hard irony in The Man's voice: "Let this be a lesson to you," he said. "Let this be a lesson to others like you."

There was the sound of one man clapping. The Man pivoted, turned, whirled, standing erect to face the sound of the applause.

There was the darkness. There were the shadows. There was the form of a man in a long coat, his hair blond, his face pale, standing above the gutted bodies of Darrin and Zach, wet blood on his bare hands black in the moonlight, those hands coming to-gether again and again in loud, solid bursts of sound. The form threw his head back and laughed, canines scraping sharp scars in the flesh of the night. He jammed his hands into the pockets of his coat as he laughed; the laughter of the tall man echoed to si-lence as he stretched the darkness of his soul across the canvas of the night and slipped away into the shadows. He left behind him the corpses of two men, the softly breathing bodies of two uncon-scious fag-bashers, the sounds of sirens hurtling toward the dark-ened parking lot, and the quiet anger of a failed hero who suddenly felt silly wearing tights.

THE PAGES SAT in the middle of a pool of light, beneath the heavy green glass shade of an old banker's lamp. They sat atop an old flat brown desk that had belonged to Matthew's grandfather, once upon a time. A computer, a small Macintosh Classic II, sat silent, its screen dark, its innards cold. A compact Apple ink-jet printer stood on the floor by the side of the desk; it too was cool, and quiet.

Adam flipped the pages, one after the other, his hand holding a red pen which raced through line after line of the manuscript. He puffed his cheeks out, he made sounds similar to farting by squeezing the red, inner wetness of his cheeks against the inside of his mouth, he jiggled his right leg now and again. In the background, an old David Wilcox CD, the first one, played the lines of the last, quiet song. He heard acoustic guitar chords, strummed softly, and the voice—a sweetly sung lament for childhood, and lost illusions.

Adam let the pen collapse on the white pages before him, and leaned back in the old wooden Windsor chair his parents bought at a neighbor's yard sale, years before Matthew had been anything more than a dream to him. He rubbed his eyes and let his hands slap the wooden arms of the chair. He looked up, toward a bookshelf: books, a white box. Adam pushed the chair back and himself up. He stretched, rubbed his hands along the small of his spine and moved away from the chair, the desk, the manuscript to stand at the window. Just before it was out of reach, he turned and switched off the banker's lamp.

Moonlight. His breath fogged softly upon the cool of the glass. He put his finger up to the window and drew a heart upon the steam, drew an arrow through the heart, made attempts at shading the heart, giving it dimensions and substance. But every stroke of his finger, no matter how gentle, rubbed away to clear nighttime outside the window.

The CD was over; the house was silent. Adam let himself sag against the windowpane, feeling the cool of the glass on his forehead, his nose, against the flesh of his arms. He closed his eyes, rocked his head back and forth slowly on its pivot against the glass and thought about crying. He opened his eyes and they were dry. He drew back to stand before the window again, drawing in a deep lungful of air, which he puffed out to cover as much of the window as possible. In the dulled reflection, he thought he could see something like Matthew standing in the doorway behind him. He turned, but no.

Adam walked from the den into the hallway, ignoring the shut door of their bedroom and walked through the darkness past the kitchen, through the living room and over to the French doors of their porch. He twisted the handles of those doors, pulled, and the doors swung open, letting night air, cold and awakening, pour over him. He strode out onto the porch and stood there, hips pressed against the flowerboxes atop the railing, hands stuffed in his pockets. His lungs filled with lungful after lungful of fresh air and Adam felt the awakened possibility in being alive.

Matthew's manuscript was calling him. Adam turned away from the night, slipping inside his house and shutting the French doors, locking them behind him. It was warm in here, and he walked quickly back to the den, where he turned on the banker's lamp and sat down in the chair. He scooted up to the desk, picked up his red pen and scanned the first few lines of type, remembering where he was and what he was thinking. He puffed his cheeks out, he made sounds similar to farting by squeezing the red, inner wetness of his cheeks against the inside of his mouth, he jiggled his right leg now and again. He worked for another hour and a half, and when he felt he had accomplished all he could for the night, when he was good and tired from the work, he let himself leave the desk, leave the den, ignore again the shut bedroom door to trail down the hallway and collapse on the comfortable, big sofa in the living room, drawing a quilt from its back atop him and cuddling up to a stuffed side pillow.

Adam slept.

CHAPTER
Four

*C*larence Smalling sat at his desk in the detective division of the City's police department. To his left, in an old, wide-mouthed Gallo wine carafe sat a bunch of daisies. In the center of his desk was his name plate and, to the right, an overflowing IN-OUT basket.

Smalling was anything but, and he took a lot of ribbing for his name. He stood six-seven. He was powerfully built from daily workouts at the gym and from pushing himself through Police Academy obstacle courses on weekends. He had dark brown hair, close-cropped on his head and his features were handsome: square and solid. He had a good smile, and he could threaten easily with the combination of a scowl and the size of his build. He was thirty-seven years old, he was married, and the fingers of his right hand now worked slowly to fiddle with, to move around on his left ring finger, the gold wedding band he wore always. Clarence Smalling loved his wife.

"Smalling!"

"Yo!"

Light fell through the large windows that lined the offices of the police department, the glass thick and veined with chicken wire. Its path lit up swirls of dustmotes, fell upon paint yellowed with age and dust layered upon desks where no one had tidied up since the building opened, shortly before the start of the Great Depression. Some of the light fell through the window to spill upon the papers Smalling was reading, the reports on what department rumor said could be a new serial killer, surfacing from increased incidents of hate crimes in the City and preying specifically on the City's large gay population. There were photos here and there, attached to each report: small squares of Polaroid film that Smalling squinted at when he came across them. There were six reports in the file.

Again the cry: "Smalling!"

"Yo! I'm over here!" Smalling recognized the voice as that of Harold Yates, the chief of the homicide division. "I'm over here, ya dimwitted, small-minded bigot," Smalling grumbled. He finished reading the last report and sat the file down upon his desk, spreading the reports out a little bit so he could see the individual names, brief corners of the photos. He bit at his right thumbnail while thinking: *Other than being gay, what do all these men have in common?*

"What the hell y'studying that for?"

Yates.

Smalling took an inward deep breath, did a fast count to ten. He looked up from the reports, turned in his chair to face his boss. Smalling rubbed for a second at his right eyebrow with his right hand. "Murder is my business," he deadpanned.

"Maybe," Yates said, without cracking a smile at Smalling's line, "but studying those reports will get you nowhere. You know tracking fag killers is impossible, Smalling. Queers're too promiscuous. Too many one-night stands. Too many unknown players." Yates' lips twisted with something now that could've been called a smile.

"You say so, sir." Smalling's fingers twisted at his wedding band again. Gold. Her. "But this isn't a killing, these are five killings, five that we can look at and see a kind of pattern to, an MO. This is something else . . ." Smalling drew it out, added it in to ease the way, ". . . sir. I think—and department buzz has it—this could be the work of one man, one very determined, confident and certain man who knows what he's doing and when and how to do it."

Silence. Then, Yates: "You 'think.' "

Again, for good measure: "Yessir, I do."

"Smalling, don't 'think.' " Yates pulled a manila file out of the IN box on Smalling's desk. "Put this crap aside and tend to business. Here. This rich bitch was sitting home when some guys broke in to rob the place. Blew her face clean off and splattered her noggin all over a Monet painting she had hanging in the living room. Husband's friends with the mayor, so this gets priority." Yates appeared to be thinking about something for a moment. He looked to Smalling, arched an eyebrow. "You should've been able to tell that, Smalling. I shouldn't've had to come over here and point it out to you."

"I've got five people here whose lives have been snuffed out, their corpses eviscerated and it's all starting to look like the work of one man."

"Smalling: one rich dead white woman takes priority over ten, twenty, a hundred dead faggots, far's I'm concerned."

Smalling's eyes narrowed into slits. "I don't think Ophelia Stern would agree."

Yates's face flared vermilion. "Ophelia Stern—and her whole goddamned Channel 7 News team—can go fuck themselves. That partisan bitch wants one thing and one thing only,"

Yates' fingers jabbed violent holes in the air between them, "and that's to see some pussy put in my office instead of a man with balls who understands that this police department is and must be a crack military unit." Yates paused, quieting; his thick finger reached out, came down to tap the folder of the rich woman. "Get to it," he said.

The two men stared at each other and Yates' lips pulled upward into a smile again as he turned away.

Smalling looked at the closed manila folder now sitting atop his IN box. He turned back to his desk, he waited until he knew Yates was out of range of Smalling's voice, until he knew Yates was sitting pretty behind the glass and wood partitions of his little office. "Kennedy!" Smalling called out.

"Yessir!" Kennedy, a detective junior grade, new to the force and placed under Smalling's supervision was at Smalling's desk, standing behind and to the left of Smalling's chair before Smalling could count to three. The kid was eager, and affable. Smalling had to work to keep himself from grinning over the man's enthusiasm.

Smalling picked up the manila folder from the top of his IN basket and handed it over his shoulder to Kennedy without turning around. "This just came in," he said. "High priority. Wife of some bigwig. I want you to take care of it for me. Got it?"

Smalling could feel the trembling excitement of the kid behind him; if the kid had been a dog, he'd've been wagging his tail all over the place. "Oh, yessir," Kennedy said. "Yessir. I'll have a full report on your desk by tomorrow morning, sir."

"Good. And Kennedy?"

"Yessir?"

"Keep this under your hat. This opportunity I'm giving you, it's just between you and me for the time being. The chief thinks you're too green to handle a job on your own but I think otherwise." Smalling swiveled his heavy wooden chair around to face Kennedy. "Don't prove me wrong."

Smalling watched Kennedy's shoulders straighten, his spine stiffen, his bearing become something certain and convincing. "I won't sir," he said. "You can count on me."

"I'm trusting in that, Kennedy." Smalling turned back around in his chair. "Dismissed," he said.

He heard the scurrying shuffle of the kid heading off to his desk to study his first packet. For a moment, Smalling allowed himself the brief smile he'd been holding back but then it faded, and he turned his attention to the photos, the reports; he began spreading them out upon the cluttered surface of his desk. Five men. Five lives. One survivor. He concentrated. The noise around him fell away into silence and in his skull he was awash in the blood spilled on backstreets.

Smalling's fingers fell upon a small plastic bag at the bottom of the folder, containing two sharp-edged metal triangles approximately three inches in diameter and painted pink. An accompanying lab report and file docket let Smalling know the triangles had been recovered from the scene of the last homicide, a double murder in a parking lot behind a neighborhood dance bar. The edges of the triangles were listed in the report as being coated with a heavy-duty animal tranquilizer whose name Smalling didn't recognize. Traces of the drug were found in the bloodstreams of the two unconscious youths found beside the corpses. Each youth bore a small nick from where the edges of the triangles had sliced into them, and here and there the dark color of dried blood still speckled the pink metal.

Smalling lifted the bag up to the light. Pink triangles: symbols of gay pride taken from the badges the Nazis made homosexuals wear in the concentration camps of World War II. The report listed the youths as having no memory, no recollection of anything that happened; they claimed to have been walking home, taking a short cut through the parking lot, when something tagged them and they blacked out. Homicide had released them after that simple line of questioning, warned them not to go anywhere. Smalling looked for the name of the interrogating officer; it wasn't one he recognized.

Smalling grunted and thought a sarcastic, *That was useful.* Smalling knew the pink triangle emblem, recognized its significance and place of importance within the gay community. But taking that knowledge, and piecing it accurately into these murders was something Smalling knew was going to take him a little while.

He set the plastic bag with the pink triangles down, off to the right-hand side of his desk, and turned his attention once more to the reports and the photos.

dam sat on the couch in his living room, his legs propped up
on the coffee table before him. In his lap he held an old
K-Swiss Classic Hi-Top sneaker box from which he withdrew
photograph after photograph, studying each one separately for a
moment, then placing it into one of the various sloppy stacks
scattered around him. He wore white socks, grey sweat pants, a
fatigue-colored T-shirt under an open pale-yellow oxford. He'd
shaved earlier that morning, he wore a tortoiseshell and gold
round pair of Armani glasses that seemed to fit his face and his
hair had gotten longer on top since Matthew had seen him last.

He pulled out another fistful of photos: Adam standing,
dressed up, before the closed white curtained windows of his parents' home, ready to head off for his junior prom; Matthew, Adam,
and Bruce, Ophelia and Elizabeth's yellow dog, standing in the

backyard of the women's home, Matthew kneeling beside the dog, Adam in the middle of saying something, holding a clear plastic cup of foamy-pale yellow beer; Adam as a child, hugging his grandmother in front of the house where they had lived, the house where Adam had grown up and she had helped watch over him.

Adam placed the junior prom photo in a stack to his right and held the other two photos before him in his hands, held them like playing cards he was considering in a game of Go Fish. The images were so different, so similar. In the one, Adam is all of eight years old, his straight black hair a sharp contrast to the light brown of his grandmother's winter coat. In the photo, he is hugging her, looking up toward the camera and she is looking down upon his head, her hands upon his back, patting, holding him. When he looks at the photo, Adam can remember well hearing of her death through the long distance wires of AT&T, his body three thousand miles away from home. Though he had not lived at home for a while when her death came, though she had ceased being an everyday reality to him in his life as he lived it, he remembers the deep blackness that seemed to soar over him with his father's voice through the wires, and he remembers crying, and holding himself in a room not so far removed from friends but far from family.

Matthew. Adam knows that he remembers Matthew, remembers him vividly but wonders if he has not already begun to move on into the living of a life without him in it. When he looks at the photo of the two of them, together with the dog in that familiar, known backyard, he can remember it all so well. He can remember standing there, he can remember sunlight catching the dark brown colors among the black in Matthew's hair, he can remember the way Matthew's voice sounded, the way Matthew's body, his back, his shoulder blades, the pressing of their chests together felt when they'd held each other in a playful hug just a few moments later, and for all of a second. This memory, this photo is of something so fresh and real, still, within his head that he wonders why no one has found a way yet to slip through time back into these split seconds of remembrance. Something as strong as these memories: there must be a way to tap into them.

But there isn't. There is the photograph, and the way Adam thinks that everything was, the way Adam's mind remembers hearing the voice of Matthew, the voice of his grandmother. The truth of those moments, though, is behind him forever, in a place he cannot get to, in a way he will only be able to tell his children about, conveying to them in singular dimension everything that ever was about these two people who meant so much to him.

His telephone rang and Adam looked around for a moment. He leaned forward, placed the photo of his grandmother in another stack to his right, while the photo with Matthew went into a stack atop the coffee table. He took his feet off the coffee table, plunked them on the ground and stood, stretching for a second before padding over the hardwood floor toward the telephone.

Ring number four. "Hello?"

"Adam?"

"Nobody but, Ophelia. How ya doin'?" Adam leaned back against the sideboard upon which the telephone sat, his left foot playing a kind of soccer with a dust bunny from beneath the furniture. The phone itself was an old, solid, black 1930s piece with a shiny chrome dial that Adam bought in a fit of pique when his Pacific Bell cordless had gone on the blink yet again. The receiver, this morning, was cold and heavy against his ear.

"Fine, okay; okay fine." The woman's voice was bright in his ear. "Are you going to be home for a bit? I wanted to stop by; there's something I want to talk to you about."

"Yeah, well sure, Oph', I'll be here but, I mean, is it something you wanna talk about now?"

"No no no," the woman said quickly, "it's a face-to-face kind of talk."

"Okay, sure, fine then," Adam said, groaning inwardly a bit. *Not another "Keep on keeping on" chat.* Elizabeth and Ophelia were good friends, yes, but they had a tendency since the accident to be a little too maternal for Adam's taste. It made sense, in a way: they had been there, from the hospital on, through everything. Still, Adam preferred the idea of standing on his own, while keeping someone at arm's length to cling to should he need them. "Come on over."

"I'm on my way."

There was a click as the line went dead. Adam hung up. He was heading back toward the sofa when there was a knock at his front door. He veered right slightly from his path and swung the door open. There was no one there, but when he looked down, Adam could see a small stack of mail upon his welcome mat, and Adam heard the heavy tread of the mailman walking away, down the steps. "Thanks," Adam said, loudly; there was only the shutting of the ground floor door in reply. Adam crouched down, picked up the mail, and stood, stepping back a little bit to close the door.

He carried the mail back over to the sideboard. Bill: gas. Bill: credit card. Bill: Matthew's credit card. New offer for a credit card for Matthew. An envelope bearing a portrait of Ed McMahon and the words: "Matthew Paul, you may have just won TEN MILLION DOLLARS!" A letter from Adam's mom. Two new comic books for Adam: *The Strangers* and *Princess Paragon*. Fab flamers and butch babes—oh my, he thought. Adam's copy of *Esquire*. The J. Crew catalog. Matthew's copy of *Friends Journal*. A manuscript packet from Matthew's publisher.

The offer for a new credit card for Matthew and the portrait of Ed McMahon Adam set aside to toss. The *Friends Journal, Esquire,* and J. Crew catalog he set aside to drop on the bathroom magazine stack next to the toilet next time he trotted in. The letter from his mother and the comic books he set aside to read after Ophelia left, and the bills he set aside in a stack he would take back to his desk. He carried the manuscript packet over to the sofa with him.

Adam sat down carefully so as not to disturb too greatly the stacks of photographs. He opened the manuscript packet, pulling at the stapled rim of the mailer, feeling the staples give way beneath his tug. He avoided their sharp points when he pushed his hand in, snagged hold of the manuscript and withdrew it. He lay the brown mailer on the floor.

He read the letter from the editor, a kind fellow Adam had always liked, easy to talk to and committed to bringing this last book of Matthew's to light. The letter was filled with thoughts, comments, introductions, some praise, and suggestions for a few further modifications that Adam would have to take a look at. Adam set the manuscript on the floor atop the mailer; all in all, it wasn't a bad letter.

Ophelia will be here soon. Adam started gathering the photos from around him and placing them neatly within the K-Swiss box. He closed the box and picked it up along with the manuscript, letter, and mailer, carrying all of them over to the sideboard where he added bills, magazines and catalog to the stack and headed back for the den, stopping briefly inside the bathroom to drop off the magazines and the catalog. He set the stack of mail on his desk, left the manuscript dead center and placed the bills in a slot of the telephone message holder that sat on the far-right upper corner of his desk just for that purpose. The box of photographs he placed on the deep windowsill behind his desk. He straightened the desk a moment, looked at it: everything seemed fine. He looked up, then, about the room, his sight casing the joint for disorder. The white box on the bookshelf caught his attention. He walked over to it, tilted his head for the umpteenth time to better read the label, his lips mouthing Matthew's name as he did so. He reached out, and with his right index finger he tapped the box, twice:

"Hiya," he said.

He turned and walked out of the den, back up the hallway, pausing briefly in the bathroom to whizz and then heading into the living room and past his front door just as someone knocked. He stopped, pivoted, swung over to the door and opened it.

It was Ophelia. "How ya doin'?" she asked. Adam stepped aside so she could come in, and he shut the door behind her.

CHAPTER
Six

*T*he curtains were drawn in the room; old yellow pull curtains whose loops hung down on their strings below the windowsills, whose plastic bodies clinked slightly against the plaster of the wall beneath the sills whenever a small breeze or movement in the room would brush against them.

Outside, Jimmy could tell it was daylight and from the strength of the light he could guess it was some time around noon. He looked around for a clock but saw none. Noon, hell; it could've been ten in the morning, or three in the afternoon, there was no way he could know for sure except by measuring the hours until night fell. He had been sleeping on an old couch, one covered in a rough fabric pimpled with shades of brown and green. He pushed himself up on one arm, rubbed at his eyes with his other fist, his fist feeling the small granules of sleep at the corner of his eyelids. He wiped at these with the flat of his hand.

Where am I?

He was wearing only his jeans. He looked around for his shirt, his socks, his shoes, his jacket, but he didn't see them. He noted a doorway behind him, open, leading further into this apartment, house, whatever. He swung his legs off the edge of the sofa and felt what was once deep shag carpeting quiver beneath his soles. He looked down. The carpet seemed yellow, grey around the pink of his feet. Once the carpet could have been a kind of gold color.

Jimmy looked around. The walls—a pale green color, the same kind old schoolrooms are that haven't been repainted since 1957—were bare of any pictures, paintings, or posters. There was no furniture in the room save the couch. There were no doors in his field of view before him; two windows on the far wall perpendicular to the couch, between the windows a small wooden crucifix ornamented with a silver metal Christ. He was about to walk over to peep past the blinds and look out when a voice from behind him asked:

"Sleep well?"

Jimmy spun about to see a man standing in the doorway, a tall man, blond, with blue eyes and pale features. He wore plain white boxer shorts that extended down to mid-thigh, and nothing else. Jimmy noted the muscles on the man, the lean strength about him. The youth compared his own body against that of the man before him, and envied the elder his physique. This man's chest was smooth, his stomach flat and hard, his legs two sturdy pistons, and his arms strong coiled springs. This man had a good body because he worked at it, because he was intent upon it; Jimmy had a good body because he was lucky, because he had been born that way. The man smiled at Jimmy in a way that failed to make Jimmy feel uneasy; more, it made him feel safe.

"Follow me," the man said. "I've made breakfast."

The man turned and headed off down the hallway. Jimmy followed him. He noted as he walked down the hallway the brown shadows around places where pictures had once hung and sunlight bleached the walls about. He tried to ask the man he followed his name but Jimmy's voice was rough and unready and nothing escaped but a dry rasp. They passed two rooms on the left, two rooms on the right, each one with a scabbed, white painted door closed tight upon it. Jimmy began to smell the smell of coffee, the odor of eggs cooking, of something like liver. The hallway opened up into a kitchen, a dining room, and the man gestured for Jimmy to sit at a table roughly laid with cracked plates and mismatched silverware. The man walked over to a Mr. Coffee coffee maker and poured out two cups of coffee, which he carried back to the table where Jimmy now sat; he handed one cup to Jimmy and took a sip from the other. The man looked at Jimmy and said, "My name is Michael."

"Jimmy," Jimmy said as Michael sat down at the table. "My name's Jimmy."

"I know," Michael said. One of his hands reached across the table for the butter, cutting off a heavy piece of it, which he slathered on top of a piece of warm toast. Jimmy watched the butter begin to melt, small rivulets of grease traveling across the nooks and crannies of the bread. Michael raised the toast to his mouth and bit into it hard, revealing to Jimmy a mouth filled with sharp teeth that severed the crust neatly. Michael chewed, and spoke through his food. "I heard your friends call to you in the parking lot, a few nights ago."

A few nights ago. Jimmy worked to remember, looking away from Michael, down and to the left. How long did that mean he'd been asleep? Two days? Three? He remembered Saturday night: he'd fucked Allison, left her, hooked up with two pals of his, they'd cornered two fags outside a bar and then there'd been that guy, the guy all in black who'd nearly beat the shit out of him and . . . that was it. That was all Jimmy could remember. Jimmy brought his eyes back to Michael's face. Michael's face. Michael's eyes. Michael watching him. Michael smiling as he chewed. Jimmy saw a second crucifix, just like the one in the living room, hanging behind Michael's head, hanging above the coffee maker. Jimmy frowned, his eyebrows knitting together in question. "How?"

"How what?"

"How long have I been out?"

"Three days. It's now a little past one o'clock on Tuesday afternoon."

Three days. "How'd I get here?"

"I brought you." Michael stood, brushed crumbs from the toast off the white of his boxers, and moved toward the kitchen stove. He opened the stove, and, using dishtowels as hot pads, removed two plates from the metal rack inside where he'd left them to warm. He set one down in front of Jimmy, who sniffed it, wrinkling his nose; Michael set a plate down for himself.

Jimmy looked up from the plate to Michael. "What is it?"

"Eggs," Michael said. He walked back over to the oven, closed the open door and turned off the gas. He walked back toward the table. "Eggs," he said again. "Eggs and kidney and potatoes." He smiled a little bit. "Try it," he said. "Try it, you'll probably like it." His smile grew a little bit broader. "It's very English." Michael sat down, pulled his chair up to the table, lifted his fork and began eating. "And," he said, looking up from his plate to Jimmy, "it's very good."

Jimmy looked at the food on his plate for a moment more before picking up his fork and digging in. Once he'd started he found that he liked the food quite a bit. The eggs were smooth, the potatoes well cooked and the kidneys like liver, only riper. Jimmy was hungry; he cleaned his plate, and Michael smiled while he watched.

•   •   •

NIGHT FELL.

"Do you like faggots, Jimmy?"

Jimmy's senses perked up through the haze of wine he had drunk with Michael while they watched the sun set through the living room windows; they had raised the pull blinds completely beforehand. *What was this?* "No, I don't like faggots," Jimmy said. He gave a laugh like a cough. " 'Less I'm beatin' the shit out of 'em."

They sat on the old green sofa, having earlier turned it so they could better watch the City, the night from the windows. No lights were on in the whole apartment; Christs in darkness. Michael smiled, and even in the shadows Jimmy could see again those sharp, white teeth. "Have you ever killed a faggot, Jimmy?" Michael's left forefinger slipped slowly around the mouth of the wine bottle. He raised the tip of that finger to his nose and sniffed: feral. His tongue darted out quickly to taste the red flavor.

"No," Jimmy said, his head wagging drunkenly from side to side, "I've never killed a faggot. Meant to, the other night when you caught me, though. Meant to kill one up good." He grabbed for the bottle of wine that Michael held; he grabbed and missed. Michael reached out with the bottle in one hand; with his other he took Jimmy's hand and moved the fingers to curl around the glass shaft of the bottle.

"Here," Michael said. "Drink, Jimmy. Drink."

Jimmy stared a soulless stare into Michael's blue eyes and then he raised the green bottle to his mouth and he drank three long draughts of the wine. When he was done, he wiped at his mouth with the back of the hand that held the bottle, the smell of the wine then again full about him. He passed the bottle back to Michael, who took it gingerly.

"Do you know why you've never killed a faggot, Jimmy?"

"Bad luck?"

"No," Michael laughed, "not bad luck." Michael leaned in

close to Jimmy's face and smiled as he said to him the words, "You've never killed a faggot, Jimmy, because you've never truly known what it means to be a faggot."

Jimmy sat on the couch with his legs open before him. He looked at Michael through a deeper haze of wine. "Are you a faggot?"

Michael laughed a full laugh, his head thrown back, and the light from streetlamps and the moon fell upon his face, the blackness of his open mouth. "No, I'm not a faggot, Jimmy. Far from it," he said, lowering his head to look at the youth. "Jimmy, I've succeeded where you've failed. I've killed faggots." He inched closer to Jimmy on the sofa. The two men hadn't showered or changed since their meal of kidneys and eggs. Michael placed his hand on Jimmy's bluejean-clad thigh and felt the tightness of the muscles there; Jimmy could see the ghostly whiteness of Michael's boxer shorts in the dark of the room. "Jimmy," Michael said, his breath hot upon Jimmy's ear, his paw heavy on Jimmy's leg, "I kill faggots." Michael's hand moved from Jimmy's thigh to cup Jimmy's crotch and Michael let loose a low growl which rumbled across Jimmy's left ear. There was a tightening, an automatic hardening Michael could feel beneath his hand; he squeezed Jimmy's crotch until the hardness was complete and then he let it go. Michael thought, Yes.

Jimmy stared vacantly out the window, seemingly separate from what was going on. Michael moved his hand slowly over Jimmy's belly and across the flat, haired sculpture of the youth's pectorals, keeping his hand always an inch above the flesh. He moved his hand in circles over each of Jimmy's nipples, and watched them stiffen as they sensed the presence of something possible. Now Michael moved to straddle Jimmy, straddle Jimmy's hips and with the one hand playing its way above the skin of Jimmy's torso, Michael's other hand moved down to cup the youth's crotch again.

The movement of car headlights in the street played across the muscles of Michael's back. He kneaded Jimmy's crotch beneath the denim. Michael's breathing was becoming rougher. "Jimmy?"

Quiet. Hoarse. "Yes."

"Do you want to kill faggots?"

"Yes."

"You cannot kill what you have not been, Jimmy." A tent-like hardness that Jimmy showed no signs of noticing began to poke its way out from the fabric of the white boxer shorts. "All hunting is begun by ritual, no matter how that ritual may manifest. The hunter hunting deer becomes the deer; he thinks like the deer, he acts like the deer, he is the deer and only when he is in perfect harmony with the deer will he be able to succeed in killing the deer." A rhythmic thrusting began surging through Michael's hips. "Do you understand?"

Silence. Jimmy swallowing and licking wetly at dry lips.

Michael's hand reached up from Jimmy's crotch to stroke the hair on Jimmy's head, to guide Jimmy's face so that the youth would look at him. Gazing intently into Jimmy's eyes, Michael repeated the question: "Do you understand?"

The youth nodded.

You do not understand, Michael thought. Michael's hand released Jimmy's head and he moved both hands so they hovered above the small stiff brownness of Jimmy's nipples. Michael looked at Jimmy, staring vacantly ahead once more, small corners of the light from passing cars slashing their way across Jimmy's face where the light had flowed from Michael's back.

Michael pinched Jimmy's nipples, hard, and twisted them sharply. Jimmy let out a cry and looked up to Michael, who back-handed him fast across the face with the clenched meatiness of a thick right fist and then a left. Jimmy bucked, his hips pulsed upward and Michael let himself be lifted clear of the youth for a moment and when Michael came back down his knees pinned Jimmy's arms to his side and Michael again clubbed him with his fists, left-right.

Jimmy yelled no. Jimmy yelled no and bucked and twisted but Michael held him fast and snaked his hand down to the waistband of Jimmy's jeans. The boy wore no underwear. Michael yanked at the denim, he pulled and there was the popping sound of the button at the waistband and then the ripping metal sound of a zipper's teeth being pulled apart and Michael's hand was inside Jimmy's pants, roving over hard cock, the sacs of his testicles which Michael found and held and squeezed, Michael's other hand grabbing onto Jimmy's hair and using it as a grip by which to slam the youth's head back against the hard wood frame of the sofa. "Shut up," Michael said through teeth he gritted hard while speaking. "Shut up, shut up, shut up!"

Michael released Jimmy's balls, released Jimmy's hair and leapt off him. Jimmy flailed away from the couch, reached for something to hold on to so he could stand and found only the sofa's arm. He used it to pull himself clear. Michael stood, silhouetted in the window, watching Jimmy crawl toward the doorway. Michael wasn't breathing hard; his tongue flicked sharply out of his mouth and an empty smile took up residency on his face.

Jimmy crawled. Michael watched. Jimmy crawled. Michael leapt, using the sofa as a vault and landing on top of Jimmy, Jimmy three feet from the door to the hallway. Jimmy kicked, and caught Michael in the chin with his right heel. Michael's head snapped back and he recovered to throw himself on Jimmy's back. His arm wrapped itself around Jimmy's throat, getting the youth in a chokehold which Michael tightened, used, squeezed until he heard that loved sound—the sound of Jesus, the sound of that other man he'd killed in the back alley—in Jimmy's throat: the bent rasping of breath past cartilage.

Jimmy stopped kicking and Michael shoved his face into the carpet, pressing the skin of Jimmy's face down tightly to the bristle and rubbing it roughly back and forth. With his other hand

Michael yanked at the back of Jimmy's jeans, tearing them from the youth and, with one swift movement, yanking them free of Jimmy's legs. Michael cast the pants aside to a far corner of the room. Jimmy's ass was hairless, tight.

One of Michael's long fingers probed its way roughly up the corridor of Jimmy's asshole. Jimmy screamed and Michael lifted his head up by his hair and slammed it back down onto the floor. "Shut up," he said. He pulled the one finger out and rammed in two; Jimmy whimpered and Michael scraped his face along the carpet.

The inside of the youth's asshole felt slick and warm to the touch and Michael wormed his fingers in deeply, watching Jimmy's shoulders tighten with the desire to buck every time Michael suddenly plunged his fingers further.

Michael pulled his hand away from Jimmy's ass and released the youth's head. Jimmy tried to push himself up. Michael reached out and yanked both of Jimmy's wrists out from under him, pulling them back, pinning Jimmy's arms behind his back. He held Jimmy's wrists together then in one large hand; the other snaked beneath the sofa and withdrew a set of heavy-gauge handcuffs, which Michael snapped on Jimmy with the rasping click of opening and shutting metal. Oh, how careful he had been when they'd turned the sofa to keep the handcuffs as a pivot in his head, keeping Jimmy unawares and yet sitting atop them all the evening. He had enjoyed that thought, tonight, knowing, as he did, their outcome, and all of this.

Michael stood up from Jimmy and told him to turn over. The youth did so, with some awkward kicking and pushing, some rolling of his body weight to get momentum. Michael was reminded of a turtle on its back.

When Jimmy turned over, Michael could see the blood. Blood from the rug burns streaking Jimmy's face, Jimmy's chest. The youth stared up at him, his face a mask of fear, his chest heaving with every panicked gulp of air.

Beautiful, Michael thought, beautiful blood. Michael smiled down at him. "Having a good time?"

Jimmy said nothing.

Michael leapt over Jimmy and disappeared down the hallway. Jimmy heard the water running. Michael was washing the smell of shit from his fingers. Then he was back.

Michael was naked. His penis stuck out in front of him, a sharp, thick spike. Jimmy watched Michael step over him, watched him walk into the room, turn around, come back to Jimmy lying there on the carpet in the doorway; Jimmy watched Michael kneel down atop him, straddling Jimmy's chest.

"Jimmy," he said, "remember: 'That which does not kill us makes us stronger.' "

"Fuck you," Jimmy said.

Michael smiled at this and moved his way down Jimmy's body, licking the blood off first one nipple and then the other. Michael licked his way down Jimmy's chest, saliva matting the trail of hair on the youth's belly. He rubbed Jimmy's cock against his face, sniffed it, nuzzled Jimmy's balls with his nose and then took Jimmy's cock in his mouth.

Jimmy let out something like a gasp and looked toward the ceiling. *What was this? Allison. Think of Allison.* He felt Michael's tongue work his shaft, the muscles of Michael's throat hard around the base of his penis. Jimmy felt the tip of Michael's tongue move about the head of his penis, felt the tingling there, the tickling sensation that was almost painful.

Just as he was about to come Michael dragged the sharp edges of his teeth up the shaft of Jimmy's cock and his mouth filled with the youth's blood. Jimmy yelled and bucked. Michael pulled away and raced his body to cover Jimmy and he placed his closed mouth over Jimmy's open, screaming one. Michael opened his mouth and the youth's blood poured back into the youth's throat and his swallowing silenced his cries.

"Jimmy," Michael said, blood smearing from his mouth over the youth's face where he left kisses, "I will make you so good, I will make you something wonderful, something whole and so complete."

Then Michael fucked him.

Then they slept.

CHAPTER
Seven

The grappling hook shot upward, trailing a tail of thick steel cable; there was the rasping catch of metal on metal as the hook caught on the uppermost handrail of a weathered iron fire escape. The cable tightened: The Man began his ascent up the alley side of a seven-story City warehouse; once at the top, he would rappel his way down to the ground.

Practice, he thought, practice. The Man's grip was firm and tight, the leather of his gloves secure on the ridges of the metal rope. The soles of his boots felt sure upon the bricks of the wall. He moved quickly to the top of the building and took a moment to walk around; his eyes staring at the ground, the sound of loose asphalt and tar beneath him as he briefly, playfully moonwalked along the building's roof. At last he looked up, toward the heavens, across the skyline of the City all around him.

Stars there, deep in the night, beyond where the lights of the City faded and the sounds of street traffic whispered up from below; The Man went to run his hand through his hair and found instead the heavy fabric of the mask he wore. He brought his hand away from his face, stared at it for a moment, the fingers, the palm, his hand sheathed in leather the color of pitch.

Stars, and the open canopy of night holding them all.

Practice, he thought now, again. *Practice.* He rappelled his way down the side of the building and was soon swallowed up whole by the night. He was headed North by Northwest, to the City's predominantly gay and lesbian neighborhood.

It was time to go to work.

CLARENCE SMALLING MOVED slowly with his wife, improvising waltz moves to keep the two of them moving in time to the soft rhythm of Sarah McLachlan's "The Path of Thorns (Terms)." His wife was pressed up against him, the softness of her breasts against the hard muscles of his chest. Her head nestled just right below his throat and he breathed in the smell of her hair, the smell of Johnson's Baby Shampoo, of sunlight with children playing outdoors, of the spaghetti supper she had prepared for him that evening, while he puttered beside her at the stove, shaping meatballs and bitching about spaghetti sauce burping droplets of red upon his forearms. He danced with her, and remembered her bending to lap the red sauce up from his arms, her tongue something smooth, wet, warm against the flesh over his muscle, the movement across the slight hair of his arms sending a shiver down his spine, which made her laugh and then he had drawn her upward and they had kissed.

Conversations of Clarence's work were *verboten* this night.

The children slept in their rooms at the end of the hallway. The music shifted "Into the Fire" and Clarence felt his wife's hips move strongly, rhythmically against his own. Her head tilted upward and he kissed her. She broke away from him moments later, keeping hold of his left hand with her right, using it to pull him down the soft carpeted hallway toward their bedroom, into their bedroom, her body turning, left hand shutting the door behind them, body close upon him once more now, mouth something fresh and familiar upon his. The music was the thin, pale pulsing of another room. Her hands ran across the broad muscles of his back; his hands slipped their way beneath the waistband of sheer silk panties, moving around, touching her, there; she was wet, and she broke away from him with a smile. "Be right back," she said, walking across their bedroom, disappearing into the adjoining bathroom. There was the sound of the medicine cabinet opening, then closing. Other sounds, and Clarence knew she was putting in her diaphragm, applying to it spermicidal jelly.

The room was dimly lit by the bedside lamp at her side of the bed. Made of weathered brass, the lamps looked like something picked up on a Native American reservation in New Mexico; Clarence knew she had ordered them from the Sundance catalog two years before. Above the bed hung a small hand-painted crucifix, the first thing they had hung in their apartment upon moving in, many years ago. It was something his mother had given him, something her mother had given her; an only child, Clarence hadn't had a sister for his mother to pass it along to and so he was awarded custody, Christ by default.

"Hi there."

Clarence turned, forgetting how to breathe for a moment, then falling back into the pattern with a lungful of air that seemed to make him lightheaded, drunk.

She was beautiful. In this light she was as the first day he met her, a woman just turned eighteen, a freshman in college majoring in journalism. She was a newly pledged Tri-Sig sorority girl; they had met at a fraternity rush party. Although he had never pledged a frat and she had taken heat for dating a God Damned Independent, their dating had been something sure and constant, carrying them through college into the real world. He had taken great pride upon seeing her byline in the college paper, a pride swelled by the fact that she was good at what she did. His chest still swelled when magazines came in with something she had written featured within the pages, when she let him read some rough draft of hers, for his opinion, to see if it was all right; as if he would know.

Her hands moved across the muscles of his chest, settling to work the buttons of his shirt, undoing them, pulling them apart, the shirt falling off his shoulders to puddle about his feet. Her hands lowered, slipping under the white fabric of the T-shirt he wore, lifting it upwards, his arms moving in compliance, her fingers grazing his chest, stiffening his nipples as they passed. The T-shirt was tossed to a corner behind him.

She undid his belt, she unzipped his zipper; the pants fell to the floor and he stepped free of them. Her hands on the waistband of his white boxer shorts, moving around to cup his balls, squeeze the hardening thickness of his shaft.

Later, when he was on top of her, her cries urging him onward, he would come inside of her, his body tensed, his eyes opening to see Christ's corpus spread before him on the wall, a pale pink triangle of shattered human flesh.

"YOU GIRLS JUST never learn, do you?"

The voice rained down on the four youngmen in the alleyway. The youths looked up to see him perched there, on the edge of a warehouse rooftop, a modern gargoyle against the round paleness of the moon.

"What the—" a stocky boy said. Three of the youngmen had gathered around a fourth, pressing him back against the brick wall of this abandoned warehouse in an alleyway not far from a popular downtown park. The fourth youngman was slight of build, with longish blond hair and delicate features. He looked toward the rooftop, and The Man, with a mixture of confusion, relief and fear.

The Man recognized the other three youngmen now. Recognized them as the ones that had first threatened him and Matthew the night they were attacked; recognized them as the ones that had first attacked the two men The Man had tried to save his first night out. *Tried to save but failed* and the thought was sour in his stomach. It's not going to happen again, old girl, he thought. *It's not going to happen again.*

He gestured toward the youngman pinned against the brick wall by a taller, lankier, pimpled youth. "Let him go," The Man said. "Let him go, and all I'll do is turn you over to the cops." The Man stood, his arms hanging loose at his sides, and waited for their response.

"Fuck you," the skinny one spat. He turned to look at the ringleader, the good-looking brown-haired kid in the denim jacket. "Pop him, Jimmy." Jimmy scowled upwards at The Man. Jimmy hefted something that glinted in the moonlight; something The Man knew as a glass bottle, broken at the bottom, jagged and sharp.

Jimmy's face hardened from indecision into hatred. "With pleasure," he said and he lurched toward the boy pinned against the wall, stabbing for the flesh of the boy's belly beneath the pale green T-shirt he wore.

The boy screamed "No!"

He fell, he flew, The Man was upon them and Jimmy found himself driven to the ground by the weight of The Man on his back, the broken bottle forced free of his grip. The surface of the alley reeked of piss and sour food. Pinned flat against the tar, Jimmy felt The Man moving atop him and he heard the cracking sound of breaking bone. He recognized the sound of Larry—the tall, skinny guy—screaming once, then crying, hollering about "my arm! You broke my fuckin' arm, you son of a bitch!" Jimmy heard the sound of footsteps, the sound of footsteps running away and he figured it was Randy, the short, fat one and then the pressure was off him, The Man was gone.

The Man tackled Randy and brought him cleanly to the ground. He straddled him, he turned him over on his back. The youngman pushed at him, swung at him, wild swings that The Man avoided easily, reaching out to snag the youngman's fists in his hands. He lifted himself up off the fat youth for a moment; when he landed back down atop him, the youth's arms were pinned beneath The Man's knees. Randy started yelling. The Man hit him once, twice in the face with the full force of his fist and Randy blacked out. Blood drizzled from his lip. The Man rose off the fat boy and turned slowly to face Jimmy, still getting to his feet in the middle of the alleyway.

"C'mere, little boy," The Man said. He started walking toward Jimmy. The Man spoke to the fellow the boys had planned to beat up, still cowering against the brick wall. "Call the cops." The guy nodded, then fled.

Jimmy looked around him, at the rubble of his gang. He looked at Randy knocked out ahead of him; he heard Larry useless and sobbing behind him. He looked at The Man, walking toward him; at the solid muscle beneath the black of the costume, the determined power behind The Man's every movement. He blinked once, twice. Nervously, quickly, he licked his lips. His hands clenched and unclenched, and his feet staggered on the ground, quick little flutter-steps of fear. Jimmy heard the sound of his own breathing loud within his ears.

Jimmy turned, Jimmy ran.

The Man ran after him.

Jimmy's feet pounded the tar of the alleyway. He ran hard, his arms pumping at his sides, his legs moving as quickly as they could; he felt a sweat break out across his forehead, his shoulders, chest and back. He was headed for the street, and the park beyond it. Fuckin' freak, Jimmy thought. On the street, he could dodge cars and turn in different directions and lose this guy in black on his tail. If that didn't work, Jimmy knew he could ditch the man in the darkness of the park.

The Man reached out and snagged Jimmy by the collar of his jean jacket, by the collar of his shirt and The Man hurled him up against the wall to his right. Jimmy slammed against it, hard, the wind knocked out of his ribcage and he sunk down to the ground, gasping for breath. He blacked out, he came to, he tried to clear his wobbly vision and regain a sense of balance within himself. The Man stalked over to stand before the youth and Jimmy's eyes came to focus upon the darkness in front of him, the darkness that had caught him; the night that would not let him go.

The Man reached down, grabbed Jimmy by his shirt front with a right fist, and hoisted him up, against the wall; to his feet, then off the ground. Jimmy squealed. Jimmy looked down to see his feet flailing in the air, hitting back against the brick of the building.

The Man asked him, "Who is he?"

"Who?"

The Man slammed him back against the wall. "Don't fuck with me, Jimmy. Who is he? The blond guy, the guy in the long coat, the guy who does the killing after you fucks have rounded up the fags."

"I don't know what you're talking about!"

"I"—SLAM!—"said"—SLAM!—"don't"—SLAM!—"fuck with me!" The Man turned, still holding the youth, and hurled him across the empty space of the alleyway to land against a row of metal trashcans that fell to the ground with a roar and a clatter. Jimmy's body lay, arms and legs akimbo, amidst the tin.

"Touch him again and you'll answer to me."

The Man spun about. "I think I'd like that."

The tall blond man stood in his long coat at the entrance to the alleyway, his face, his body obscured by shadow. Behind him, a car passed by on the street, oblivious. The Man couldn't see what, if anything, the tall man held in his hands; The Man heard Jimmy let out a small groan.

"Jimmy," the blond man said softly, "come to me."

There was a clattering of metal as Jimmy pushed trash cans away and raised himself on wobbly legs to lean against the brick of the wall. He reached up with his hand to rub the back of his skull. "My head," he moaned. "I hurt."

"I know," the blond man said, his voice still quiet. "It will be all right. Just, come to me."

"I am."

"Like hell," The Man growled. As Jimmy stumbled past The Man grabbed him and held him against his own body in a chokehold, a hold he tightened until Jimmy sagged against him, unconscious. The Man let Jimmy down softly to the ground, then stepped over the boy's body. "Come and get 'im," he said to the tall man. The Man's hands balled into fists but his arms kept loose at his sides.

"No, come and get me," the blond man said, smiling. He spun about to disappear around the edge of the alley.

The Man hesitated. He knew the blond man was gone. He knew chasing after him was pointless. He heard in the distance the rising sounds of police sirens and he believed he should be as far away as possible by the time the cops got here. He remembered the boy in the pale green T-shirt he had rescued this evening from these attackers. The kid would be fine; scared, probably edgy for a little while, but fine. The Man looked at Jimmy, still passed out on the ground; he, too, would heal. He looked at the empty space at the mouth of the alley where the blond man had stood, in his long coat. He looked past the street, to the park beyond.

The Man turned, leaping over the fallen bodies of trash-cans, and clambered quickly up the brick wall, disappearing into the night. Beneath his mask, The Man was smiling.

Next time.

CHAPTER
Eight

Adam stared at his empty bed for a moment. It was unmade, the white sheets sprawled across a mattress still covered tightly by its fitted sheet. He slapped lightly at his chest with the palms of his hands, checking the pockets of the jacket he wore for pen, for wallet, from habit. He turned and walked out of the room.

In the hallway, beside the key basket, he paused for a second to check out his reflection in a mirror. Everything looked all right: hair freshly short-cut; jacket still pressed enough, its navy blue clean-looking against the white dress shirt he wore; the pale brown of khaki pants. He jammed his right hand into a pants' pocket for keys, found none; checked the key basket, found some, scooped them free, and resettled them in that right pants' pocket. He stood there for a moment, his hands stuffed in his pockets. He shrugged and listened to the muffled jingle of the keys.

He turned from the mirror and headed for the front door, the hard soles of his shoes making clop-clop noises upon the hardwood floors. He bent to pick up his gym bag by the door; he left quickly. There was the light rattling sound as he tested the locked door behind him; there was the damp thudding sound of rapid footsteps as he trotted down carpeted stairs toward twilight air.

HE WATCHED THE WATER run down the smooth planes of Sanchez's body, the wiry muscle beneath brown flesh. He watched the water glisten across the pale scar on Sanchez's torso before rushing lower, across the curves of pale buttocks and the darker flesh, the dark hair about the youngman's genitals.

Adam looked up to Sanchez's face. Sanchez was smiling at him. Adam smiled back, somewhat sheepishly; took water in his mouth from the shower, and spat it toward a drain in the center of the room. He looked back to Sanchez, still watching him; Adam smiled again, rubbed soap to a lather between his palms. He smeared the bubbles across his chest, across his neck and up, finally, over his face. Eyes closed, he stood beneath the hot spray of the shower and let it wash him clean. He turned around and let the water relax his shoulders, his neck; his head bent, his arms folded across his chest. Eyes still closed, he spoke to Sanchez: "Hey, can you teach me a few kick-boxing moves?"

"Sure."

"Thanks."

"But why, man? I mean, how come you wanna learn to kick-box?"

" 'Cause Jean-Claude Van Damme's so hot."

"No, really."

Adam opened his eyes to respond but Sanchez had already turned off the water of his shower and was walking away from him, toward the dressing area. Adam saw the line of Sanchez's back, the tightness of his ass.

Adam got a hard-on. He turned around, wrenched off the hot water and steadied himself against the wall of the shower.

BRUCE BARKED IN RESPONSE to Adam's knock upon the white painted door. Adam stepped back from the door half a step and waited. He could hear Elizabeth's voice from within saying, "Coming, coming," and the nearing sound of her footsteps upon the hardwood floor of their hallway.

"Coming, coming," said the voice again from behind the door; then there came the sounds of a small, excited tussle and the words "Bruce, no, please, back up, just a little, Mommy needs to—" The door swung open. Elizabeth stood there smiling up at Adam, her body bent over slightly, one hand holding on to Bruce by his collar, her other hand upon the doorknob. "Hi, Adam," she said. "Come in."

Adam stepped inside; Elizabeth shut the door and released the yellow dog, who wagged his tail furiously and barked twice at Adam before running off to fetch Ophelia. "Bruce!" Elizabeth yelled after him. "Bruce no running in the house!" She turned to Adam. "If only they listened like children."

"I thought they did."

Elizabeth smiled again and then they stood there for a moment, in the hallway, the rest of the apartment spanning out behind them, Adam's hands jammed again into the pockets of his khakis, Elizabeth's arms crossed across her chest, a hand coming up now to tuck away a strand of black hair.

"So," she said.

"So," he said.

Bruce barked from somewhere deep within the women's dwelling.

Elizabeth unfolded her arms to gesture toward the sound. "I guess Bruce—" She stopped, as if unsure how to continue. Then, "Ophelia should be ready, soon." Again the smile for Adam. "Her turn to run late, this time. You want to go back and see her? You want a beer? Anything?"

"Sure," Adam said. "Sure." He pulled his hands from his pockets as he followed Elizabeth back through the apartment toward the kitchen. Her hands were washed in cold light as she reached within the refrigerator to withdraw the amber Amstel bottle. She held it tight for a moment, used the edge of a close towel to buffer her grip as she twisted off the cap. She handed it to Adam with a "Here." He took it, feeling against his palm the sweat rising on the surface of the brown glass. He said, "Thanks," and raised the bottle to his mouth to take his first sip.

Then again, for his second.

A third.

The words fell out of her in a small, startled rush. "Adam, look, I know this is awkward for you, I know this must be awkward for you. It's awkward for me." Elizabeth paused in her speaking, her face downturned, eyes watching the pale yellow, pale green linoleum tile floor of the kitchen. She looked up at Adam, who was watching her, who was waiting. "Maybe we never knew each other all that well. Maybe Matthew kept us buffered, in a sort of way, from each other. Maybe we, I don't know, depended upon him too much to be the link between our two households."

"He was." Adam took another drink of beer.

"I know, I know." She made chopping motions with her hands now, her left into her right. She was leaning back against the countertop. She looked away from him then, back down the hallway they had just traveled. "It's just that we've missed him, you know? Ophelia and I, we've missed him, and it's hard. For you"—she took a deep breath, and again there was that sudden onrush of words—"I don't know, for you, it seems like it might even be easier for you, in a way. He was a part of your life, your everyday life, and while that makes it harder and perhaps more painful, I can't help but think, it also makes it clearer, somehow. More insistent. With us, with me, with us, it's like we're just between dinners, is all. Sometimes. Like 'Tomorrow he'll call; I'll talk with him tomorrow.' " The words slowed from her. "But we won't." She looked at Adam again. She bit at a corner of her lip. "He won't. . . ."

Adam took a last swallow of his beer; he began picking at the edges of the label, trying to peel it off the glass. At last he looked at her levelly. "I don't know what you want me to say."

"Ready to go?" Ophelia stood in the doorway. "Hi, Adam." She came over and gave him a good, solid hug, even as Elizabeth slipped away behind her for the bathroom. Ophelia pulled back from Adam yet kept her hands upon his shoulders. She looked straight at him when she spoke: "It's good to see you." Behind them there was the sound of running water from the sink tap in the bathroom. Ophelia's left hand moved to stroke gently the right side of Adam's jaw. "It's been too long," she said softly.

He blinked at this, and drew her close to him for another hug. "Ophelia no," he said. "Ophelia, it hasn't been long enough."

THE LIGHT SHONE DOWN in the center upon the room, upon the metal of a table and three shadows along its edge resembling chairs. In three of the darkened corners of the room there stood the bodies of men; waiting, silent and watching. A man walked around the table. A youngman sat at the table. A square foot of glass, veined with chicken wire and set into one of the walls at a height of six feet from the ground, glowed with light from the outside hallway. An intercom sat on the wall nearby.

The man walking around the table paused before the youth sitting at the table. The man standing gestured for the other three men to leave and they did so, their exit a heavy sound of weighted belts and the thudding echo of a shared weary tread. As they approached the door, their faces shone in the light from the square foot of chicken wire; when they opened the door light flooded the small room, blinding the boy sitting at the table until the door closed and he could blink once, twice to restore something of his sight. He shook his head. He looked to the man standing before him.

That man reached out and cuffed him, and Jimmy felt his head knock back and to the left from the blow. A small bit of blood began to bubble at his lip and his tongue darted out to taste of it. He bit at the sore spot, making more of the blood flow into his mouth, blood tasting thick and warm, blood he swallowed.

"What the fuck did you think you were doing?" Harold Yates leaned into the circle of light covering the table, one hand upon the table, one hand upon the far armrest of the chair holding Jimmy. He leaned in close to Jimmy's face. Jimmy could smell Yates' breath, could feel the heat in Yates' face from his anger. "I asked you, what the fuck did you think you were doing?"

"Nothing!" Jimmy started, then fell back into his chair, sullen. His finger sketched a circle upon the tabletop. "I told you, we were just out, hanging, when we got jumped."

"Bullshit."

Jimmy stared at Yates. Yates stared at Jimmy. Yates straightened and backed away from the table, began walking again in shadow around the room. "I haven't talked to you in three days, haven't seen you in five and you turn up in some back alley with the shit kicked out of you. Larry's got a broken arm, Randy's nose is broke and you're still sitting there telling me you were just hanging out when you got jumped?" Yates screamed the last two words.

"Yessir."

"Bullshit!" Yates came quickly about the table and grabbed on to the back of Jimmy's head, the back of Jimmy's jacket, turning the boy's head to the side and slamming his face, the upper part of his chest down upon the table. The metal echoed like thunder in Jimmy's ears. Yates spoke through clenched teeth. "What were you doing out in some back alley at that time of night with those guys?"

"Nothing!"

Yates picked Jimmy up a brief bit and then slammed him loudly back down onto the metal of the table. "What were you doing?" he slammed

"Nothing!"

—him again. "What were you—"

"Nothing!"

"—doing?" And again.

"Nothing! Stop it," Jimmy said. "Please." His voice softened; he was whimpering. "Daddy, stop it. Please."

Yates backed off. Jimmy sat up from the table, rubbed at his face with his hands and wiped the wetness away from his eyes. He sniffled.

"Stop crying, you fucking pussy." Yates' words hardened Jimmy. Yates stood in a dark corner of the room, his back to the table, his arm reaching out to prop himself up against the wall. His other arm rested at his hip, upon his belt. His voice was quiet. "What were you doing out there, Jimmy?"

Silence; breathing then "Nothing. Beating up fags, that's all."

"What?"

"Beating up queers. You know."

Yates turned and walked back toward the table. He leaned down to stare at Jimmy levelly. Jimmy stared back. "Fag bashing?"

"Yessir."

"You and your buddies were out fag bashing when you got jumped?"

"Yessir."

Yates: "Listen to me, you little shit." Yates' finger stabbed the air before Jimmy's face, his eyes. Jimmy didn't flinch. "I'm the chief in charge of homicide in this town and it doesn't look so good to have my kid talked up as a fag basher."

Jimmy stared down his father. "You telling me you don't like what I did?"

"I'm telling you I don't like you getting caught. Jesus! I've got people on my ass in this place about the kind of thing you're talking about. Christ! Do you know how much Ophelia Stern would love to find out that my kid was running around beating the shit out of queers last night? Seven o'clock news, hello, she's got her local Emmy and I've got a whole new ball game to deal with." Yates backed away from the table, moved to stand in the corner. "Did you even think about that? About what your running around could do, to me?" He turned. "To us?" His voice softened. "To our family?"

In his head, Jimmy laughed.

Yates changed tack. "So how'd you get beat up?"

"Some guy."

"Some guy?" Yates moved in closer to the table again. "A faggot beat you up?"

Jimmy shook his head, "No," then shrugged. "I don't know. It was just some guy, all right? Some guy all in black, in this costume-like thing." Jimmy paused. He jiggled his right leg nervously; he bit at a fingernail while he thought. "We ran into him once before."

Yates' face furrowed with questions. "When?"

Jimmy looked to his father. "That night Larry and Randy got picked up and said they were jumped."

"The night those two queers got killed by the bar?"

Jimmy nodded slowly.

"Did you . . . ?"

Jimmy shook his head.

"Did Randy or Larry . . . ?"

Jimmy shook his head.

"Did this guy all in black . . . ?"

Jimmy shook his head.

"Do you know who did?"

Jimmy nodded, slowly.

Yates pulled out a chair and sat beside his son. "So let me get this straight. You and your buddies go out fag-bashing and some guy in black comes along and stops you, not once but twice. Still, there's someone else out there who's actually doing the killing, someone who's not this costumed wanna-be, but someone who's getting away with it."

Jimmy nodded again.

"And this costumed wanna-be is trying to stop you from hurting those guys, he's trying to protect the faggots, is this right?"

Jimmy shrugged, then nodded once more. He looked to his father and his father was smiling. "This guy you know who's actually out there doing these killings, do you know if. . . . Has he killed before?"

"He killed a coupla queers seven or eight months ago. I know 'cause Larry and Randy and me had already flushed out the two guys."

"Where?"

"Near Washington Street."

Yates tapped his finger upon the table. "If it's the incident I'm remembering, he killed one man then."

Jimmy didn't follow. "No, I'm pretty sure it would be two. There were two, two of them and I remember because we caught them walking up the street, holding hands and talking all this other gay shit and then they ran for it." Jimmy shook his head. "No, Daddy, there were two."

"Yeah, there were two, Jimmy, but your friend—this guy— didn't kill both of them." Yates' finger tapped the table as the memories fell together in his head, and his eyes began to gleam with excitement. "Yes. This is it. Two men were attacked in this particular action but only one of them died. One of them lived, one of them got better. I remember because Stern made such a big fucking deal about it on the news. This incident was what really gave her the leverage to swing out all that hate crime bullshit. It pissed me off. She chased after me for a while before letting it slide . . . for now." Yates basked his countenance in the light of the ceiling lamp. "Jimmy, Jimmy, Jimmy."

The chief of homicide for City Police reached into the pocket of his shirt and pulled out a Polaroid photograph. He slapped it down in front of the lad. "Recognize this guy?" Father looked to son.

Jimmy looked at the photo. It was the youngman they had cornered earlier that evening. The pale green T-shirt he wore was ripped and soaked with blood, as were his jeans. He'd been gutted. Jimmy mouthed a few words, his eyes locked onto the image of the picture.

Yates asked him, "What?"

"That's him," Jimmy said, and he looked up. "That's the guy Larry and Randy and me cornered tonight."

"Thought so." Yates stuck the photo back in his shirt pocket. "Just came in," he beamed. "A sidestreet not far from where they picked you guys up. Your friend has apparently been quite busy this evening." Yates leapt up from the table, crossed the room to an intercom and buzzed to have Detective Smalling sent down in twenty minutes. He returned to the table, to the light, and to his child.

"Jimmy," he said, "let's get our stories straight, okay boy?"

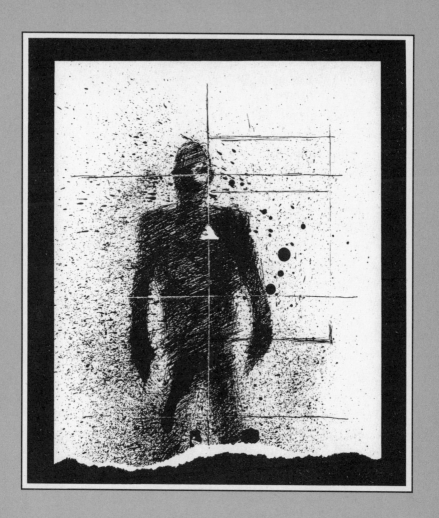

CHAPTER
Nine

*A*dam stumbled into the car next to Ophelia, who settled herself behind the steering wheel, fastening her seat belt and pressing the key into the ignition. She motioned for Adam to fasten his seat belt and he did so, clumsily, tugging at the heavy fabric, fumbling with the metal clip. "Thanks for bailing me out." He shook his head, he yawned, he rubbed his face. "Thanks for the Channel 7 attorney."

She started the car. "Not a problem. Give one of Keith's kids an 'A' sometime, if you ever go back to teaching." She looked over her shoulder and began backing the car out of the parking space. "What time did they come to pick you up?"

"Two-thirty. I'm sound asleep and BLAM-BLAM-BLAM! this pounding at the door, and it's 'Clarence Smalling, City Police Department. We have a warrant for your arrest.' Pants, shirt, and shoes later, I'm in cuffs and on my way downtown for killing five people and beating the shit out of myself." He shook his head; he stared out the window at the passing night streets. "Motherfuckers." He rolled down the window and tried to let the night air cool him off.

Ophelia reached out and patted his leg. He jumped, then looked to her and said "Sorry. Ever since I got beat up I've been all twitchy, all tingly and weird feeling, in my muscles, in my head sometimes."

" 'S okay." She paused, turning the car onto a street that would eventually pass Adam's front door. "It was a stupid arrest. They should've known medical reports would show you couldn't've inflicted that beating upon yourself." Her face darkened. "Let alone what happened to Matthew."

Adam sat sullenly, the light from passing streetlamps flickering over his face. "I hate everything."

They drove on for a bit.

"Did you hear the news?" Ophelia glanced to Adam.

"What news?"

"They have an artist's rendering of the guy they think is doing the killing."

"They had that eight months ago."

"No, this is something different. It came in while you were being questioned. It seems the guy who worked you over has gotten a little slicker, started dressing up since you guys got hit."

Adam looked out the window absently, and annoyed. "What?"

"Yeah. Smalling gave me a copy for use on the news tomorrow—today—and I can't wait. It's the first new bit of news we've had in a while, and it's good. I can let people know what to look out for, what to call in."

"Yeah, yeah, that's great."

"You're a bitter, self-absorbed old queen, you know that?"

Adam glowered at her. She smiled at him. She reached into

a folder beside her and pulled out a sheet of paper, slightly crumpled. She handed it to him; he took it.

"Of course, we'll have a better copy for the actual show but that's my copy to work from." She shot a glance at Adam, grimly studying the piece of paper in his hands. "What do you make of it? Pretty out there, huh? Notice the pink triangle?" She shook her head. "I don't get it."

Adam looked at Ophelia. He blinked. Ophelia looked at Adam. Adam tucked the sheet of paper back into the folder between them and leaned his head back against the headrest of her gold Beemer. "I'm tired," he said, "I need to go to sleep."

They drove the rest of the way in silence.

CHAPTER
Ten

*T*hree weeks later Jimmy sat waiting in a car, his body slouched behind the steering wheel. He was halfway through a Marlboro; two cigarettes were left in the partly crumpled red and white soft package that sat atop the car's dashboard, a black plastic Bic lighter lying beside them. The car was an old Dodge Dart, with peeling black vinyl roof and fading green paint rusted off here and there in patches along the bottom. The end of the cigarette glowed reddish-orange; blue smoke escaped Jimmy's lips a second later, filling up the air inside the car. A cheap plastic rosary and a Playboy car deodorizer hung from the rearview mirror. He wore an unbuttoned black plaid flannel shirt, its long sleeves rolled up to his elbows; a white T-shirt, well-worn pale grey corduroys and sneakers: ragged black Converse hightops.

Other cars drove past Jimmy, the light from their headlights reaching past the glass windows of his car to stroke their way across him, only for a second, before moving on. Jimmy's car radio was silent. There was no sound to be heard other than the crunching tires of passing cars over the loose gravel of the alley, the raspy exhalation of smoke from Jimmy's lungs. It was three o'clock in the morning. Jimmy was parked in an alley behind the Adam and Eve Adult Bookstore.

Jimmy rolled down his window, flicked out the cigarette, and let his last lungful of smoke out into the night air. It tasted sour passing his lips; he licked at them, he swallowed. The yellow light spilling out from the open rear door of the bookstore illuminated roughly half the shop's parking lot, casting the edges of the lot, the walkways on either side of the bookstore into shadow, the building buttressed on either side by other buildings, storefronts: private retail establishments open only during the day. Jimmy hung his arm out the car window and dragged the inside edge of his thumb slowly back along the smooth surface of the car door. He counted three cars parked in the small Adam and Eve parking lot. Three cars, all of them old, none of them worth much: an old Chevy Malibu, Jimmy couldn't make out its color in the light, but it was probably a rusted kind of dark blue; a black beat-up and boxy old Volvo; a yellow VW bug.

He gasped, he jumped in his seat a little when his hand brushed against something solid, something warm.

"Hi."

Jimmy looked up, his gaze traveling across a denim-clad crotch, a black leather belt, a black leather vest—shiny where the light hit it as it draped across the leatherman's well-muscled chest— and finally toward a handsome young face, clean-shaven, square-jawed, with close-cropped brown hair and deep-set eyes Jimmy found nearly impossible to see except for the occasional glint.

Jimmy nodded.

The leatherman's voice was deep and clear: "What's up?"

Jimmy shrugged. His hand had begun to shake. He swung it upward, he rested it on top of the open window to keep it still. Jimmy could feel his heart pounding in his chest; he worked to keep his breathing even.

The leatherman's hands moved, but only slightly, in suggestion. "Mind if I get in?"

After a moment, Jimmy shook his head no.

Jimmy could hear the softer crunching of the leatherman's boots upon the gravel as he walked around the back of the car. Another car passed by them, slowed, was ignored, drove on. There was the deep clicking sound to Jimmy's right of the door handle being pulled, the sound of the door opening; a momentary shifting of the car's weight and the leatherman was inside the car, the door was shut, the night was quiet.

"I'm John."

"Jim—" he stopped and shook his head, briefly. "Jake," Jimmy said.

The two men shook hands, their eyes meeting across the bit of open seat space between them. When their hands separated, the leatherman let his drift down to rest atop the muscles of Jimmy's leg; he felt the leg tense beneath grey fabric worn thin.

Jimmy could feel the leatherman's eyes watching him. Jimmy turned his head so as not to look at the leatherman, so as not to look at the leatherman's arm where it reached across the empty space between them. He turned his head so as not to look at the hand resting warm atop his thigh, the fingers of the hand strong, kneading their way into the muscles of Jimmy's leg.

Jimmy could feel himself starting to stiffen, the blood thickening his shaft and making him uncomfortable. He was awkwardly positioned inside his trousers, bent over upon himself, it seemed. Jimmy's right hand moved quickly, darting beneath the waistband of his pants, beneath the waistband of his Fruit-of-the-Loom jockeys, taking hold of and straightening out his cock.

He pulled his hand free of his crotch and already John's hand had moved upward, settling to rest from Jimmy's thigh upon the hardening length now lying along the crease between Jimmy's hip and leg.

Jimmy saw no cars were coming. The same three empty cars sat undisturbed in the parking lot.

Jimmy turned his head slowly. Jimmy looked over at John. Jimmy's stare rode over the ponderous bulge in the leatherman's crotch, the well-muscled smoothness of the leatherman's chest. Jimmy's voice was even when he spoke: "Want a cigarette?"

John nodded.

Jimmy reached for the cigarette package on top of the dash, grabbed it, and shook the two cigarettes into his free hand. He crumpled the now empty Marlboro package into his fist, enjoying the feeling, the sound of crushed cellophane and paper forming into a ball that he shaped briefly by rolling it between his palms. He let the ball fall to the floor. He stared down at it for a moment, watching it come to rest by his right foot upon the black rubber floormat of the car, watching as it expanded for a few moments, then lay still.

Jimmy looked over to the leatherman and grinned. John grinned back and Jimmy let himself laugh for a moment, a short, harsh laugh that snapped Jimmy's head back with its sound and silhouetted him against the light from the bookstore.

Jimmy rolled the cigarettes together between the palms of his hands, evening out the tobacco. He put both cigarettes in his mouth, he lit them with a single hit from the lighter that had been next to the cigarettes. He took one of the cigarettes from his mouth with his right hand, and he held it out to John, who bent, his eyes closing, to take it into his mouth. His head bent low, John's eyes closed, his mouth close about the mottled tan filter tip of the cigarette.

Jimmy brought his elbow up quickly and slammed it hard

into John's jaw, feeling the snap of John's head as it was thrown back, hearing the sharp biting noise of John's jaws snapping shut. The cigarette fell to the floor. John had been thrown back, away from Jimmy, into a far corner of the front seat. John had bit his lip and now he reached up with his hand to dab at the warm blood he felt, the taste wet and bitter in his mouth. His eyes were wide as he looked at the blood on his hand, as he looked to Jimmy and said, "What the—?"

But Jimmy was on him, lunging across the empty space of the car seat until he had the leatherman pinned in that far corner of the Dart, Jimmy's body weight holding down most of John, pinning his arms and legs, with Jimmy's elbow pressing tight up against John's throat. Jimmy pushed with his right arm then, pushed back further until he heard that sound, the rough sound Michael had told him about, the sound that Michael loved, the sound of dying, the sound of God, the sound of life's breath being given, then taken away.

Jimmy looked into John's eyes, the frightened, trapped animal he saw trying to escape there, and Jimmy smiled pleasantly at him.

Jimmy brought his left hand up slowly and slapped it down tightly across John's face. Jimmy blocked the vision in the leatherman's right eye with his palm; Jimmy used his fingers to hold John's left eyelids apart, and kept them from blinking. Jimmy could feel the slight pull, the reflexive tug as the lids tried to shut, to close; protect.

Jimmy took a slow, deep drag on the cigarette clenched between his teeth. The end of the Marlboro burned hot, burned red; burned hotter, burned orange. Jimmy sunk this end of the cigarette into John's opened eye.

John made a noise like a scream but Jimmy's right arm kept the leatherman's jaw shut and so the sound was muffled. Jimmy pulled away from John's face slightly, leaving the cigarette embedded in the leatherman's eye. Jimmy pushed back with his right arm until he could no longer hear the sound of that rough breathing Michael so loved. There was a final tenseness, a final holding of the leatherman's neck before the sound like a fistful of spaghetti breaking in two. Then there was just the looseness of John's head upon his shoulders.

Jimmy heard the sound of approaching footsteps upon the gravel and asphalt of the alleyway. Jimmy glanced through the windshield of the car and saw a man walking towards him, slowly, an older man wearing a windbreaker and with wispy hair upon his balding head. This man was backlit by the headlights of a car that had just turned into the alley. Jimmy hunched himself over the leatherman's body as the man drew nearer, Jimmy's mouth on top of the dead man's mouth, Jimmy's crotch grinding against the corpse's now permanent hard-on. This discovery made Jimmy smile. *I knew you liked it, queer.* Jimmy's hand slipped to press against the leatherman's midsection, and dead air leapt from the leatherman's lungs to fill Jimmy's mouth with its stale flavor. Jimmy heard the footsteps of the man pause at the car, then move on. The car too passed by.

Jimmy sat back. He gave himself a few moments to let his breathing even. He remembered, he bent down, he looked around between John's legs, splayed there from the car seat, and he found the cigarette he had proffered to John still burning on the floor, on John's side of the car. Jimmy reached down, he lifted the cigarette from the rubber mat, drawing it up from between John's legs and into his mouth. He took a long hit off the cigarette. He took it from his mouth; he turned it so he could look at the lit end, and he laughed as he breathed out the blue smoke that had filled his lungs but now dissipated, escaping through the open car window into the night.

I did it. I killed a faggot.

He grinned. He was on a roll. Jimmy looked over to the bookstore, to the same three cars still parked there.

He got out of the car.

He went inside.

It was four-thirty a.m. when the ring of the telephone echoed down the hallways, echoed in the rooms of the home of Clarence Smalling, and woke him from his slumber.

CHAPTER
Eleven

*A*dam walked through a police department already buzzing with the day's activity at seven-thirty in the morning. The smell of burnt coffee hung in the air. Here and there, Adam could also smell the sugary fried sweetness of doughnuts, chewed on the run, devoured at a desk, the white confectioner's crumbs brushed away with annoyance from the papers of files or the ticking of suits. Curtains of morning light fell from tall windows lining the far wall. Caught in one of those curtains, hunched over at his desk, recognizable from the occasional newspaper clipping on heroism and a well-remembered cameo at Adam's front door in the wee hours of the morning a few weeks before, Adam saw the broad shoulders of Detective Clarence Smalling. Smalling flipped over one piece of paper, started reading another; Adam could see that the pieces of paper had photographs attached to them, shining in the light, in the upper-right-hand corners of the pages.

Adam made his way across the room, weaving between desks and trash cans and errant rolling office chairs before coming to stand before Smalling.

When he saw Adam, Smalling stood, his arm reaching out to gesture for Adam to sit in the chair to the left of Smalling's desk, his hand reaching out to shake Adam's hand. Smalling's grip was firm, and Adam winced a bit. Smalling noticed this and Adam said, "Worked out too hard at the gym this morning," with a low voice and the start of a sheepish grin.

Smalling nodded. He sat. Adam sat. The fingers of Smalling's right hand twisted nervously the wedding band on his left. Adam noticed the movement and almost let out with a short, friendly bark of a laugh. *Nice emblem of heterosexual privilege y'got there, cop.*

Smalling realized Adam was watching the movements of his hand, the fingers twisting the gold metal. "Nervous tic," he said.

Adam was smiling at him. Adam winked at him. "Gotcha."

They sat in silence a few moments, the noise of the office, of typewriters and whirring printout machines; of ringing telephone and conversations half shouted, half heard rushing to fill up the air between them.

Adam coughed, clearing his throat, and rubbed at the corner of one eye before speaking. "Ophelia Stern tells me you're one of the few decent cops around here, the only one she can count on to give her the up-and-up."

Smalling shrugged, looking up toward Adam for a moment, then looking away, looking at the vast office stretching out behind them. "I try."

"I want to know why you came to my house and arrested me three weeks ago."

Adam's voice had been quiet and kind; gentle, not angry. Smalling's right index finger picked at a drawer edge on his desk.

I feel guilty as hell about that, Smalling thought. He watched the finger, the drawer edge as he spoke. "I was told to. The Bureau Chief—"

"Yates?"

Smalling nodded.

"Fascist."

Smalling nodded. "Yates came to me, told me there was new evidence on the series of hate crimes we've been tracking in the City."

"Why you?"

Smalling looked up at him. "I'd been wanting to move on this for some time. Yates had bitched me out for working on it before but three weeks ago he got all gung-ho on the subject. Came at me with new information, a new witness—"

"Who?"

"Don't know." Smalling resumed his picking at the desk drawer, but not before glancing over to the glass office in which Yates sat, his back to them, working. "Yates said the guy wanted it kept quiet, said he'd only come forth if his identity could remain a secret so it didn't ruin his career, his life. Yates said the guy was married, a conservative career field. . . . He intimated that maybe the guy was a politico of some kind."

Adam made a dismissive motion with his hand. *Fucking closet-case losers.* Adam leaned in. "So then what?"

"Yates wanted to know if didn't it seem funny that you had survived when everyone else who'd been attacked by this guy, or this gang, had been killed. Yates told me that this witness-guy told him to check your alibis for the nights in question, said that you had thrown yourself in front of that car to cover your ass, to make it look as if you too, were a victim."

Smalling said nothing else. Another glance at Yates' cage said that he was up from his desk, prowling about the confines of his office. Adam's eyes tracked Smalling's glance and then the two men looked at each other with an understanding, a shared sense of complicity.

"You look tired," Adam said.

"Got called in at four-thirty."

"That new suspect drawing you have is bullshit."

Smalling shrugged, then nodded.

"That whole 'new witness thing' is bullshit, isn't it?"

Again Smalling nodded. "I think so."

"You knew when you busted me that it was bullshit too, didn't you?"

"I did, and if it's any consolation or apology, I'm sorry about it." Smalling tensed, then relaxed, letting out a small, brief exhalation of air. Yates was at his desk again, his back once more to the men. "Yates likes to run this place like a junior-grade boot camp. Part of that means that if Yates says do something, you do it. He usually leaves me alone, but on this one, he's got me pegged out and there's not a whole lot I can do about it except go along and try to beat him at his own game."

"Can you?"

"I better." Smalling left the corner of the desk alone, finally. "You know what this city is like for anyone who isn't part of a white 'traditional' family with a household income of thirty-five thousand dollars or more." Adam nodded. "I have my limits, but Yates hasn't crossed them yet. I'm smarter than Yates, but he's awfully, awfully cunning, and quick."

Adam crossed his legs; made a rubbing motion with his left hand across his chin. "Ophelia tells me you've got a nice wife."

"I do. I'm lucky that way."

"So was I." Adam stopped, thought about what he'd said and added, "I'm sorry. That sounds bitter, and I don't mean for it to."

"But you are."

"But I am." Adam nodded. "I am." Adam looked up to the

ceiling, the peeling paint, and exhaled before looking back to the detective. "Am I in the clear, here?"

Smalling fiddled with a paper clip on his desk. "Far's I'm concerned, yes; but technically, no. I'd keep someone around as much as possible to make sure you've got an alibi should Yates get another bug up his ass after a killing."

"Have you guys increased your patrols in the City, in those neighborhoods where these things have gone down?"

Smalling hesitated. Smalling shook his head.

"Are you going to?"

Smalling shook his head again. "Having this guy fall into our laps is a priority; keeping him from killing again is not, so long as we can look like we're busy and trying to do something."

"For Ophelia Stern and her Channel 7 News team?"

"For Ophelia Stern and her Channel 7 News team."

Silence sat between the two men again. Smalling finished mangling the paper clip and he leaned back to toss it away into his trash can. As he settled into his chair he looked at Adam, the man's well-muscled six-foot frame coiled there in the chair before him, the man's stare focused on nothing more than the empty white blankness of the tall windows behind Smalling's desk. Smalling cleared his throat, and Adam looked to him sharply, quickly, his eyebrows raised in curiosity.

"Mr. Morgan, has anything more come to you from the time you've had to think about what happened to you"—Smalling backpedaled with his words, trying to soften them somehow—"to you, and Matthew, and what's happened since: the other incidents; the newspaper reports; even this guy Yates talks about in a black bodysuit? Anything that could help us?" Smalling leaned in closer to Adam. "Anything that could help me?"

Adam looked at Smalling, looked away to the white panels of light behind Smalling's desk. *The tall man stroked Matthew's hair with his left hand, absently; ran his hand along the leather sleeve of*

Matthew's jacket. He took the edge of the pipe and played it along the line of Matthew's jaw, Matthew's mouth, Matthew's nose, his eyes, his brow. Adam's fists clenched themselves against the end of the chair's metal armrests. The steel bucked beneath his grip.

Adam looked back to Smalling, and blinked away water. *Tell him.* "No," Adam said, "nothing. I remember nothing more than what I told you when it happened." He paused, breathed. "I'm sorry."

Smalling's voice was soft. "It's okay," he said, but Adam wasn't listening to him anymore. Adam's gaze had loitered away from the desk and presence of Clarence Smalling. Adam had glanced across the other stacks of paper, the other manila folders resting upon other desks, the other officers working, typing, talking on the telephone, or flipping, as Smalling had been doing before Adam arrived, through sheets of reports with shiny photos attached. Adam had looked at the glass cage in the middle of the room, at the man sitting inside it, and then across the room, toward the doorways, where he saw the blond boy enter the room, the blond man crossing the room, weaving familiarly through the desks, the trash cans, the errant rolling chairs.

"Who's that?"

Adam nodded with his head toward the blond youth approaching the doorway of Yates' glass cage and Smalling shook his head thoughtfully, relaxing, a kind of smile starting on his face, the same kind of smile strangers get when approaching universally common areas of smalltalk. "Yeah. That's Jimmy, Jimmy Yates. Chief Yates' son." Smalling watched Adam watched Jimmy. "Why?" Smalling asked, the possibility of a smile fading. "You know him?"

Adam shook his head no, "No." He looked over to Smalling; now it was Adam's turn to smile, tightly. "No, I don't know him at all." Adam shifted about in the chair and made ready to stand. "I should probably be going." Adam stood.

"Thanks for coming by," Smalling said, his attention focused upon Jimmy, and Adam's question for a moment longer before realizing Adam was standing, was ready to go. Smalling leapt to his feet, stuck out his hand. Again, the two men shook hands; again, Adam winced. "Take care of that arm," Smalling said.

"I'll do that."

Adam had stepped free of the chair and turned away from Smalling's desk when Smalling stopped him by asking, "Mr. Morgan: two questions?" Adam turned to look at the big man. "I'm just curious: why'd you come down here this morning?"

Adam paused. He fumbled with the pockets of his jacket, after a moment pulling out a wadded, torn-out newspaper clipping. "I read this over coffee this morning," he said. He spread the clipping out on Detective Smalling's desk, unfolding it across the paperwork and Polaroids to a back-page story of four men murdered on or about the premises of an adult bookstore in the City known to be frequented by homosexual men. Smalling looked at the clipping for a moment. His shoulders sagged, and Adam noticed again the weariness that hung about this man. *Four-thirty.* Smalling looked at Adam, looking at him. "I was crashed out on Ophelia Stern's couch when it happened," Adam said. "Don't worry."

Smalling nodded absently. Smalling's broad hands played across the newspapers, feeling the other papers, their photographs scattered beneath.

Adam waited. "You said you had two questions?"

Smalling looked at Adam as if he didn't understand the language the man spoke. He blinked, once, twice, then nodded. A faint smile began to play about his lips. "I wanted to ask you," he said, "I wanted to ask you how you were, these days."

"I'm fine," Adam said, "now. These days—" he looked toward the glass cage, at what appeared to be a heated father and son discussion taking place inside. "These days, Detective Smalling, I'm better than ever."

And he waved good-bye before turning to walk away from Clarence Smalling, the still-bright curtains of morning light, and this police station.

HE WAS STANDING there when she opened the door, hair plastered to his forehead from the rain outside, T-shirt wet across his chest.

"Jimmy," she said.

"Allison."

She swallowed and reached up to toy with the buttons of her shirt collar, nervously tugging at them, pulling them together. She was aware of the sound of rain beating against the tin roof, against the east, the northern walls of her trailer. It was evening.

"May I come in?"

She mumbled "Sure," and stepped aside while he entered. She shut the door behind him and moved to stand away from him, away from his body. She stood upon yellowed linoleum, in the middle of the kitchen.

"Got a towel?"

She started. "Yeah." She gulped at the words. "Yeah. I'll, I'll be right back." She turned from him, easing past him and fleeing into the hallway leading back toward the trailer's bedroom, a bathroom, the linen closet. "Make yourself at home." The words were hollow, echoing out from the darkness of the hallway, and Jimmy used them to start himself circling about the living room, his fingers playing across the smooth woodgrain finish of the small television, her bookcases; across the rough fabric of the couch. He wiped at his forehead with his fingers, clearing rainwater from his brow. He flicked the water off his hand and the water made small dark splotches upon the pale beige of her living room carpet. He looked up toward the ceiling, at the white pegboard there.

"Here," she said, holding out to him a terrycloth towel of faded burgundy. "Here."

He reached out for the towel, his stare now locking into hers, catching her. She trembled, stopped, trembled again. As he took hold of the towel he moved his hand so that his forefinger would brush against her palm as she pulled her hand away. He watched her flinch at this. She wiped her pale hands on the red fabric of her pants. He smiled. He dried his hair.

She walked backwards into the kitchen.

Jimmy reached down and grabbed the bottom of his T-shirt in both hands. He pulled upwards, tearing the damp cloth from his body. He balled the cloth up in his hands and tossed it so it landed by the couch.

Allison reached out and placed her hand atop the counter.

Jimmy smiled at her. He ran his hands across the muscles of his chest, the slight hair there, following its line low, across his belly. He shook out the towel, looked at it, found a dry part, and rubbed it across his chest, his back, the muscles of his neck, his armpits. He tossed the towel so it landed by the couch as well. "Got a T-shirt?"

She stared at him. She shook her head no.

He walked toward her, stopping at the border where linoleum met carpet. His voice was low: "Allison."

Again, she shook her head, no, and he stepped from the carpet onto the linoleum, his arms rising up, his hands reaching out to grip her shoulders. He rubbed at the sockets of her shoulders with his thumbs; he looked her up and down. "Allison," he said, and moved in to kiss her. "Allison."

She shut her eyes and felt his lips upon hers. She could feel the physical warmth of him, the cold rain evaporating from his body to steam about her. She stopped breathing; she waited for him to finish, to pull his mouth away from her mouth.

He didn't.

She opened her eyes. His eyes were open. Her eyes widened at this; he squinted as his eyebrows came together in a moment of bewilderment and then his eyes brightened with anger. His grip on her was tighter, his mouth pressed upon hers harder, and his tongue pushed its way past her teeth until it pressed up against the warm thickness of her tongue. She swallowed spit; he breathed into her. She tried to say his name. She waited to feel him hard against her.

His fingers worked clumsily at the buttons of her shirt and then his hands were rough, fumbling, clawing at the spaces between the buttons, taking hold of the edges and ripping the fabric apart; tearing the shirt from her with fast movements, it felt, of his fists. He wrenched her bra from her the same way, in an awkward fierce pulling of elastic and cotton. The metal back snap gave, and he let the bra fall, with the shirt fragments, to the ground.

His mouth found her nipple and he sucked on it, bit at it with his teeth, his hands working her other breast roughly enough, she knew, to leave red welts when he was finished. Still she waited to feel him hard against her, rubbing himself along the length of her legs the way he used to do, the way he'd always done, every time they'd done

this.

But he didn't. Instead he stepped back away from her. His face was flushed, his breathing ragged. The muscles of his body, his chest, his stomach, his shoulders were tight and hard.

He reached out and slapped her.

She fell to the ground, with the shards of her clothing, and tried to cover her face. He cuffed her, knocking her hands from her face and then he slapped her, again, before falling down on top of her and pinning her to the cold floor.

He was rubbing against her, but she could feel no hardness on him there. Nothing pressing itself against her, just the quick sliding movements of his legs upon hers.

He pulled back, rearing off her, and yanked open the zippered fly of his Wrangler's. He pushed at them, pulled at them, drawing them low enough so that they hung about his buttocks, freeing up his crotch.

He pulled down his underwear with one hand and took out his limp cock with the other. Shaft in his grasp, he placed his other hand at the back of her head. She started to shake; she closed her eyes.

"Open up," he said. He thrust his hips forward.

She felt the head of his penis pressing against her lips and clenched her jaw against it:

No.

He rubbed the length of his penis, its shaft, the head, against her mouth, across her face. Still he was flaccid against her; still she kept her mouth shut, her eyes closed:

No.

He lifted off her for a moment then she felt his body weight slam into her once again. His hands were tearing at her pants now; she felt the button at the top of the fly, the zipper itself giving way. He was pulling her pants down, he was pulling her panties down, his fingers were probing down between her legs, feeling for wetness; she was so dry. He was moving himself about on top of her, shifting his weight, his position. He was moving his hands, his fingers were down there, between her legs and he was opening her, he was inside her, no, it was his fingers, he was moving he was trying to stuff himself soft inside her.

She could still hear his breathing, harsh and loud, and she could still feel his fingers working with her, working with him until the fingers left her and the breathing silenced and there was nothing but a silence for the moment, and his weight atop her.

A fist slammed down hard upon the linoleum, hitting the ground to the right of her skull and it slammed itself down repeatedly, the blows causing the floor beneath her to move, to shake. The fist hit the floor five times. She started crying. He rose off her. She could hear him getting dressed. She stopped crying, tried to silence herself; she was afraid of making him angry. She started shaking; she tried to stop that too.

She waited. *Please God, let him leave.*

"I'm not a faggot."

She heard his voice, hoarse and rough. She felt his tread upon the floor of her trailer as he walked across the carpeting of the living room. He was headed for the door.

She heard his hand turn the knob.

"Allison, you fucking ugly bitch. If I can't get it up for you, you think any man can?"

She heard the door open, and beyond his presence in the doorway there came to her the smell of fresh rain.

"I'm not a faggot." She heard the door close, she heard his footsteps moving down her few stairs and then along the walk, away from her trailer. And she heard now, again, the tapping of the rain upon her roof, the brushing of the water against the sides of her home.

Allison curled herself up into a ball upon the hard floor of her kitchen, surrounded by the remnants of her brassiere and shirt, red pants down about her ankles.

Allison cried.

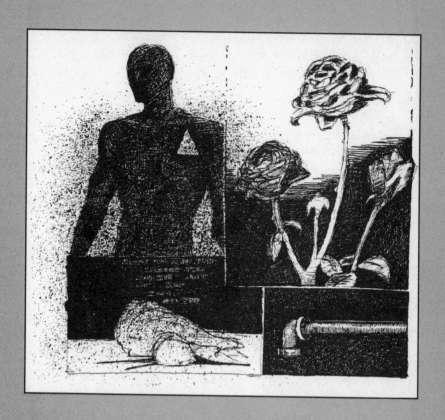

CHAPTER
Twelve

*T*wo weeks later, Ophelia chopped celery in Adam's kitchen, her brown hands moving the silver of the blade swiftly through pale green vegetable flesh, the sharp metal grazing lightly now and again against pale brown wood. She pushed the celery aside, drew a tomato to her from a small mound of vegetables to the right of the cutting board; silver against red and small seeds with water everywhere. "What time did you say he was due?"

"Any minute." Adam scurried past her, his fingers fumbling nervously with the knot of his tie. He pushed at it, pulled at it, gave a dissatisfied grunt before pulling it apart. He stood in the middle of the living room, his fingers wrapped in silk, smoothing out the cloth before trying the knot again.

Her voice came from the kitchen. "And how did this get set up?"

Adam, to himself, "I don't know," and then, to Ophelia, "At the gym. Boxing. We boxed for dinner. He beat me." Adam's fingers felt about the knot, smoothed the tail of the tie against his chest. He said it irritably: "It was his idea." Adam moved to stand before a mirror and shrugged his shoulders to let the white shirt settle about his shoulders, watched the tie settle against the valley of his pecs, his belly. He moved his fingers to play with the edges of his shirt where they tucked into his pants.

A low wolf whistle echoed from behind him. He turned to see Ophelia smiling in the doorway of the kitchen, her arms folded across her chest, her face creased with a smile, "Girl, you is bee-yoo-tay-ful."

Adam shot her a look of ironic thanks that was not without genuine appreciation. He crossed the room to where she stood and hugged her, her arms moving to hug him, her head buried next to his chest, his nose smelling the shampoo she washed her hair with that morning.

"Thanks for letting us use your apartment. I can't believe our VCR went on the fritz the one night we'd been planning to watch that *Le Coeur Découverte* flick you swore we had to see."

She felt him breathe, then speak. *"Mi casa es su casa,"* he said. *"Mi VCR es su VCR."*

Ophelia patted his back lightly. "You speak lousy Spanish, you know that?"

"Sí."

"I'll leave leftovers in the fridge for you." She felt Adam shrug a dismissive "It's no big deal." She waited a moment, listening to the rhythms of his breathing, his heart. "Have you gone out with him before?" He could feel her voice against his throat, and she felt his reply dry in his mouth before washing into the air.

"No."

Her hand rubbed his arm. "Have you gone out with anyone, anyone since. . . ."

"No." Adam's voice was muffled against the top of her head. He gave Ophelia a quick kiss there and stepped back, letting her go. He looked at her. She looked at him. He smiled. She smiled back.

The doorbell rang.

They both started. Adam again tucked in the blousing of his shirt; he squared his shoulders, he smoothed his tie.

Again the doorbell.

Ophelia looked at him, her expression one of suggestion: "You want me to get that?"

Adam shook his head, no; turned and walked over to the door. He opened it.

Detective Clarence Smalling stood there, his body filling the narrow landing of the hallway. "Mr. Morgan," he said, "may I come in?"

"Sure." Adam nodded and stepped aside. Smalling entered, his presence as heavy in the large room as it had been upon the landing. Smalling blinked when he saw Ophelia. His eyes opened and shut to the timing of Adam closing the door. Ophelia shifted her body weight from one foot to the other.

Smalling noticed, and asked Adam, "Is this a bad time?"

"No," Adam said, coming to stand between the man and the woman. "No. You two know each other." Adam lowered his voice to parody basso profundo introductions of important people one to another. "Ophelia Stern, this is Clarence Smalling. Clarence Smalling, Ophelia Stern. Channel 7 News, City Police Department. City Police Department, Channel 7 News." Adam ran his fingers through his hair while Smalling and Ophelia shook hands.

"Adam's all nervous, see, 'cause he has a date, Detective Smalling," Ophelia nodded, and Smalling enjoyed watching the light of familiarity come on in her eyes.

"Want a drink?"

Smalling shook his head no, his hands copying the motion before him. "Can't." He saw Adam shake his head gravely, almost

135

knowingly, Ophelia too, and so he added, "It's not that I'm on duty or any of that TV kind of thing. It's actually more that I'm pretty much off duty, and due home in a bit." A goofy grin crossed his face as he looked from Adam to Ophelia and back again. "I'd rather not play with the kids while smelling like a rummy and all."

The three of them stood there for a moment, letting Smalling's grin die away and they moved to sit in the living room: Smalling and Ophelia at opposite ends of the sofa, and Adam in a chair he turned out from the writing desk.

Smalling launched in. "The reason I'm here is kind of embarrassing but I don't really see any way around it." He directed his attention now wholly to Adam. "Last night, late—early this morning—they brought in someone, some guy. Drunk he was, then, picked up around Fifth and Spring and yapping about how he was goin' around making the world a better place by 'offing queers.' " Smalling winced at the word, looked apologetically to Ophelia and Adam. "Sorry. His term." The large man shifted his weight on the sofa before moving on with his story. "The reason why I'm here is, they've decided they want to see if they can make anything this guy says stick.

"You, of course, come into this because you're the only one we've got who can identify this guy . . . the guy . . . the guy who beat up on you and your partner."

Adam nodded.

Smalling continued. "So the upshot of all this is that they want you down at the station tomorrow morning first thing to make a positive ID."

Adam steepled the fingers of his hands before him, his gaze darting to Ophelia's open countenance, then back to the detective. "But you don't think it's him."

Smalling looked to the ground. "No, I don't. The guy that hurt you, the guy that's behind all the rest of this shit, he may be a lot of things, but I doubt he's some skid row drunk."

"Me too." Adam stood, walked over to the bookcase, used his finger to trace a line of dust off the frame of a photograph Elizabeth had taken and that she and Ophelia had given as a gift to Matthew and Adam two Christmases ago. The surreally developed naked bodies in the photo were of the two men. He didn't look up from the framing when he spoke: "If I can't ID this guy, will they let him walk?"

Smalling shrugged. "Probably."

"Lotsa queers get 'offed' every year. Who's to say . . . ?" He let the question fall away unformed. He lightly pounded his fist upon the wooden bookcase shelf; he turned around to face Smalling and Ophelia. "I know," he said to Smalling, "I know what you're thinking. Those streets you named, the streets where he was found. This guy isn't a killer, this guy is a drunk looking for a lifetime supply of state-provided three daily squares, and nothing but." Adam moved to sit in the chair at the desk again. "Drunks don't kill people unless they get behind the wheel of a car." He looked up at Smalling: "Yeah, I'll go downtown tomorrow. Yeah, I'll take a look at the guy, and if it's him then yeah, I'll ID him for you."

"Thanks; that's all I need." Smalling unfolded his bulk from the couch and stood. His presence filled this room of the apartment, and Adam thought he could feel it pressing about the walls, straining against the planking of floor and ceiling, squeezing all the air away from this, his home. "I'll be on my way. Go home, y' know. Play with the kids. Kiss the wife."

"Sounds idyllic," Adam said.

There was the smallest of pauses but then Ophelia and Smalling filled the time with niceties. She showed him to the door; goodbyes were traded like junk bonds. The door opened and shut and to Adam, the apartment appeared almost buoyant, so filled was it with light and air in the wake of Smalling's departure.

Adam was brooding. Ophelia watched him for a moment

until he realized she was watching and he said, coldly, "I don't want to talk about this."

There was a knock at the door.

"All things considered, that's probably just as well." Ophelia turned her back to him and walked off into the kitchen.

Adam lifted his hands up to cover, then quickly rub, his face. When his hands fell to his side, his face was flushed; red. From the kitchen, there came the noise of Ophelia again chopping vegetables: swiftly, and with determination. Adam's hand felt cold upon the doorknob.

He turned it, he pulled.

Sanchez stood there, grinning at him, his youth resplendent in white shirt, blue blazer, khakis and loafers. "Mr. Morgan," he said, "long time no see. How ya doin'?"

Adam smiled at the question, at the man. He stepped aside so Sanchez could enter the apartment.

ADAM AND SANCHEZ walked shoulder to shoulder along the sidewalks leading back to Adam's house. They'd had dinner at a pleasant restaurant, old and established, the food plentiful and heavy, the wine resting thick in their consciousness. The conversation had been light and general: talk of familiar shared ground (the gym), talk of family histories (Sanchez was a second-generation Mexican-American, Adam a first-generation-by-virtue-of-adoption American white European mutt), talk of the food, of the wine, of the City, of why they had started boxing (Sanchez had two older brothers who had always picked on him because of his size; Adam had Matthew, and that night in the alley).

They turned to walk up the courtyard path of Adam's apartment building. At the doorway to the stairwell, they stopped, turned; they faced each other in light pooled about them from streetlamps, washing down across them in a yellow bath drawing moths to play about its uppermost source. There was the smell of roses soft about them, white and red flowers blooming from a trellis that climbed this side of the building.

"So," Adam said.

"So," Sanchez said.

"Here we are."

"Here we are."

"You gonna invite me up?"

Adam raised an eyebrow at the question, looking at Sanchez, at his smile, his beauty. And Adam slowly, regretfully, and with a sagging of his shoulders shook his head, no.

They stood there. There was the sound of a moth fluttering against the lamp; a block away there was the wet sound of car tires rolling by.

Adam leaned toward Sanchez.

Sanchez leaned toward Adam.

Adam reached out and placed his hand atop Sanchez's heart, feeling the separation of blazer and shirt. He could feel the warm musculature beneath the fabric; he could smell the wine of supper on Sanchez's breath. He pushed, slightly, and the men stopped their leaning. "Arturo," he said, and fought against the desire to get lost in the sweet brownness of the young man's eyes, "I'm sorry. I can't." He let his hands move about to pat down the lapel of Arturo's blazer. In Adam's next breath and its release they both felt the ending of the moment shared, an opportunity swimming by and away from them.

The two men stood there a moment, staring at each other. Arturo shrugged finally and said, "Okay."

"Okay?"

Arturo smiled. "Okay."

Adam reached out and pulled Arturo to him in a bear hug, growling happily at the secure feeling of holding someone close to him, this way, again. He kissed the man on the neck before drawing back, clapped him once, twice on the shoulders. "Good night. You walking home, or driving?"

"Walking. It's—I don't live far." He lent Adam a quick smile. "G'night." Arturo turned and walked away, back down the courtyard path, turning to walk up the street they had traveled moments earlier.

"Walk safe!" Adam called out.

Arturo waved without looking back.

HE LOOKED AT HIMSELF in the mirror on the back of the bedroom door.

He smoothed his hand across the fabric of the mask covering his face, the vague shadows upon it cast by the outcropping of a nose, the hollows of eyes, of mouth. The hand continued down, across his throat and the blackness there, playing its way south, across the broad planes of his body, the pink triangle badge over his heart, the fingers lifting when touching, running over the rise about his waist for the belt and, there, the pink metal triangles.

He watched all this in the yellow light of his bedside lamp.

He stepped through the open bedroom window onto the tarpaper surface of a roof. Moonlight washed him in silver and he looked upward, toward the moon, toward the points of light that were stars, toward the light of a jet plane swiftly passing above: a silver ship sailing on a sea of inky air.

His boots made scratching noises upon the tarpaper as he walked. There was the roof's edge, the edge of the moonlight; darkness sweeping its way below him.

A swift fog rose up about him, and he swam away into the night.

SANCHEZ WALKED QUICKLY along the nighttime streets of the City. The penny loafers he wore made clop-clop noises against the cement of the sidewalk. He passed from pool of light to pool of light, a new-settling mist softening the streetlamp's glow. He walked near the curb; he kept clear of the edges of dark alleys and shadowed doorways.

He turned to take a shortcut down a street of favored houses in the City. One block long, the street held houses originally built in the early 1800s. A precursor to the row homes that lined some of the later, more graceful City streets, these two-story houses rested atop cavernous basements and generation upon generation of history. The current owners of these houses had lovingly restored them, painting them, the outside colors of grey or pale yellow finding contrast in black shutters and iron grillwork across entranceways and first-floor windows.

An alley bifurcated the short street, and the whole of the block was lined with thick-trunked shade trees that massed together at the top, forming a kind of protective border, separating the street from the sky. In the summertime, in the daylight, residents gathered to sit in the shade of these trees and talk about the weather, or the neighborhood; the changing events of their lives. When night fell, the residents moved inside. Supper was served, discussions continued, and the hours of network prime time passed. Then the neighbors went to sleep, dimming yellow light in window after window along the block; they made love.

And after that, in the smallest hours of the morning, bodies would begin to line the street. Moving from the thickness of a tree trunk to stand against a lamppost, moving slowly up the alley toward the main street, toward passing cars eager to slow, to take in the youngmen emerging from the darkness; loping strides carried the bodies of the hustlers from this street to shadowy back entranceways where furtive gropings transformed themselves into rent and utility bills and the morning coffee, tomorrow's supper.

Sanchez walked down the middle of the street. At this hour, not yet midnight, the street looked deserted, and Sanchez strolled happily along, his hands stuffed in the pockets of his khakis. He whistled "Maria" from *The Sound of Music* quietly to himself, segueing when finished into "Maria" from *West Side Story*. He scuffed his feet lightly against the cobblestoned surface of the street, enjoying the noise his shoes made. He was five houses into the block, approaching the lip of the alleyway, when he saw a rustling in the shadows beneath the trees from the corner of his vision.

He turned his head to get a better look. There, beneath the shadow of the second shade tree past the alley, was a vagueness assembling itself into a youngman: a youngman in sneakers, jeans, and an unbuttoned plaid flannel shirt, stepping from the shadows of the tree and into the backlight of the street ahead of Sanchez. Moonlight turned the youngman's hair into a halo; Sanchez couldn't see the boy's face in the night.

Sanchez stopped his walking. He took his hands from his pockets and let his arms hang loose at his sides. He felt a creepiness fill the air about him. He felt an electricity running through the muscles of his body, quivering in his flesh and setting his skull to itch. He felt his hackles raise.

The youngman stepped forward into the light. Sanchez could see, beneath the open shirt, small dark etchings of hair upon the muscles of the youngman's chest, shadowing his abdominals in a disappearing line to his crotch. Sanchez felt the electricity in his body twitch about the muscles of his hands, bunching up in the flesh of his shoulders, the tightening of his stomach. His mouth tasted something sour and dry and empty.

A lead pipe cracked Sanchez across the back of the head. He fell forward, carried by the force of the blow, his chest collapsing against the cobblestones, his cheek pressing against their cool, wet surface.

Michael stalked a path around the perimeter of Sanchez's body. He outlined Sanchez until he came to stand beside Jimmy; gently, he nudged the youngman in the ribs: "Pick him up."

Jimmy stood still, his body wet in the yellow light, his thumbs hooked into the pockets of his jeans, edging their way beneath the flannel shirt. Again, Jimmy felt the pipe nudge his ribs, harder this time, and this time he flinched. But he didn't move. He swallowed from a dry mouth. His tongue flicked out and licked his dry lips. *This one was mine.* "What'd you do that for?"

Michael said nothing.

"I said, 'What'd you do—' "

"I heard what you said."

Silence. Car tires passing upon pavement a block away. The sputtering of a streetlamp which went to black above them, a rosiness starting from its center.

"Pick him up." Each word was said slowly, deliberately.

Slowly, deliberately, Jimmy pulled himself away from Michael. Jimmy circled Sanchez to stand on the other side of Sanchez's sprawled form, his right foot by Sanchez's left hand. He squared his shoulders, he stared across the space of Sanchez's body, and Jimmy told Michael, "No."

Michael breathed in, breathed out. He looked upward, seeking out stars in the nighttime left by the burned out streetlamp. He held the pipe before him, secure in his hands, the length of it bumping gently against his crotch.

Jimmy watched Michael, Jimmy counted to ten, feeling the sweat build on his palms and forehead, feeling his need to blink increase.

"Jimmy," Michael looked down from the stars, "pick him up."

"I said 'no,' " the words appeared only as shapes upon his lips and he cleared his throat, he said them again.

Silence. Time.

Michael leapt across the space that separated them, his weight crashing into Jimmy and driving the boy down to the ground. Michael sat atop Jimmy, Michael's legs pinned Jimmy's upper arms, Michael's body weight kept Jimmy from bucking and kicking him free. Michael slammed down the pipe. Jimmy twisted his neck and the pipe clanged against cobblestone. Michael raised his pipe, brought it down again; again, the ring of metal upon stone. Michael stared at Jimmy, watched the boy gulp in air through cracked lips, watched the fear rise in the youngman's eyes.

Jimmy stared at Michael.

Michael smiled. Michael took the pipe and lifted it above Jimmy's head, Michael gripped the pipe in both hands and Michael brought it down slowly, watching the rising fear spill over from Jimmy's eyes, watching the begging in the form of his name start to issue from the boy's throat, watching the boy shut his eyes and twist his neck but there was nowhere, really, to twist to.

Jimmy felt the lead cold against his skin, felt the metal pressing against the cartilage of his throat. The sound, the roaring of blood within his ears, the fire of breath within his lungs; Jimmy felt it all. He roughed out a pleading whisper: "Michael."

Life was delivered back into him with the release of the pipe from his neck, with a strangled cry from Michael and the lifting of Michael's weight from Jimmy's body. Jimmy rolled right, away from the direction he had felt Michael's body go in leaving him. Jimmy propped himself up on one arm, he coughed, he pushed himself to his feet, he staggered, he caught himself, he looked, he blinked, he rubbed his eyes.

The Man landed a swift right to Michael's gut and followed it with a quick left, then brought his fists together and raised them to clip Michael sharply on the chin and Jimmy watched Michael's head snap back and he saw The Man lean into him and bear Michael to the ground.

The pipe shone, grey metal in a gutter on the other side of the street.

Jimmy went for it.

Michael's fist reeled up and connected with the side of The

Man's head but he did not let go, The Man did not lift free of Michael. The Man flailed for the hand Michael had used to strike but his flailing missed and another roundhouse punch caught The Man in the face and he stood, he stepped back. Michael rose to drive his right shoulder hard between The Man's legs.

The Man's left hand swept down to grab Michael by the hair of his head; his fingers yanked, tightening upon Michael's hair, and he pulled Michael away from him, he spun Michael blindly out toward the side of the street where Jimmy stood, toward the side of the street where Jimmy stood holding the pipe; toward the pipe.

The Man fell back into the shadows.

Michael glared at Jimmy, a hot, angry stare that made Jimmy step away from him, instinctively made the youngman back away from Michael with blood spilling down his chin from a split lip.

"Here, Jimmy, Jimmy." Michael's voice was rough, hovering about the edge of human. "Give me the pipe, Jimmy."

Jimmy stepped back further. He was aware of the alley three, four paces behind him. The alley, the houses lining it, their backyards, their safety, their refuge, escape—

"The pipe!"

Jimmy bolted for the alley, his hand flinging the pipe at Michael, Jimmy's body turning, Jimmy's eyes not bothering to stop and see if the pipe had hit the man. The boy's sneakers skidded as he turned from the wet cobblestone of the street onto the asphalt paving the alley and his arms swung out, but he caught himself, he kept his balance. The sound of his sneakers slapping the tar echoed throughout the small space of the alley. Jimmy passed backyard after backyard; Jimmy was heading for the main street ahead of him, for other people, for safety in numbers.

The pipe caught Jimmy square on the side of the skull as he ran from the alley onto that main street. He crumpled instantly and Michael was upon him, the pipe swinging down and once more and there was blood, there was brain, there was flesh and face and the pipe slamming down again and again and again then there was stillness. Michael's shoulders sagged. He reached up, he hoisted the pipe clogged with gore aloft toward the heavens and he cried, he let out a sound that brought clouds to cover the stars.

The cry overtook The Man in the shadows of the sidestreet, his shape crouched protectively before the still-unconscious form of Sanchez. The cry filled The Man with a primal fear that he shook off and afterward, there came back to him the water-washing sound of car tires spinning over asphalt an alley's length away.

HE WATCHED AS the lights went on in the apartment, he watched the shadows play upon the walls, the form passing about the lights within the rooms of the apartment. He watched the lights go out one by one in the apartment, and he watched the apartment as it sat in silence, in night.

He watched, and he waited.

CHAPTER
Thirteen

*H*e pushed the chair out of his way with enough noise to make Smalling look up from the paperwork spread out upon his desk. The place between Smalling's eyebrows creased as he watched Adam Morgan march toward his desk. Adam Morgan was moving, fast. Adam Morgan was pissed.

Adam stood at Smalling's desk. "I just got frisked by two of your lesser bozos-in-blue down at the front desk," he jerked a thumb back toward the doorway. "Your boss hate me again or something?"

"Kind of. Yates' son was killed last night." Smalling shook his head, turned his hands upon the folders on his desk. "Bad news. The good news, such as it can be, is—" Smalling looked up at Adam. "I don't know. Maybe there's something to Yates' idea that the guy who beat up you and Matthew's now running around the City in black hose and a mask. Maybe Yates' witness isn't entirely incredible. Yates seems to suffer no doubt but that guy killed his kid."

Adam folded his arms across his chest. "So am I your number one suspect again? What? You have some kind of fucking Mardi Gras get-up in your desk drawer there so I can strut about while you see how comfortable I am in black fucking Underalls and a mask?"

"No." Smalling drew out the word, not letting himself smile at the picture Adam's words had painted for him in his head. The detective spun his chair back far enough from his desk that he could lean, his hands clasped behind his head. "Well. Jesus, you're uptight."

"I have reason to be."

Smalling arched his eyebrows.

"You call me down here to ID some drunk that we both know isn't the killer of my partner"—Adam sagged down into the chair by Smalling's desk—"and I get treated like a criminal as soon as I walk into the building. I come up here, and along with finding the customary mere ineffectiveness of our city's finest I find that even you've gone over the edge and now everybody's running after 'Batman' in the City's back streets." He shifted in the chair. "Don't mind me. I had a rough night."

Smalling leaned across the corner of his desk to Adam. "Mr. Morgan, remember: Yates isn't your normal guy. We're talking about a man who grew up on *Commander Cody* serials. This guy's running around the City in black, that's all Yates knows: black is bad, white is good."

"Interesting multi-cultural slant you got here," he drew it out, "really. I'm sure Ophelia would jump up, turn around, pick a bale o' cotton to agree."

Smalling, irritated, raised his eyebrows at Adam. "That isn't my opinion, Mr. Morgan. You oughta fuckin' know that." Adam stared at him; Smalling stared back. Adam nodded, Smalling spoke. "You ready to go look at these guys?"

"Yeah."

"Great."

"Sorry."

"Me too."

The glass cage was empty.

ADAM UNPACKED GROCERIES from two brown paper sacks set upon the countertop; a third rested, waiting, on the floor. He stuffed canned goods into shelf after shelf of the open cabinets above the counter, the whole while spinning about, avoiding the twisting turns of the white spiral cord connecting the receiver, pinned between his shoulder and his ear, to the telephone on the wall.

"Of course it was useless, Ophelia, of course it was. The guy wasn't there. Buncha drunks. Lousy rummies."

Chatter from the other side of the conversation. Adam opened the freezer door, threw in three Budget Gourmet side dishes and let the door shut on its own behind him. He buried his head into the top of one of the other bags atop the counter, "Uh-huh . . . uh-huh," and he pulled away from it, his hand reaching in to draw out two bundles of celery which he placed in the refrigerator's crisper. He stared at the vegetables behind the brown tinted plastic: "Ophelia, did you ever wonder why celery was bound up by something as rusty as those wire twistees you use on garbage bags?" He let the refrigerator door shut, he went to root in the bags some more. "I mean, this is food, for chrissake. That's garbage. Aren't there poisons—something, anything—rust from the metal?" He stopped rooting, sighed, and turned to lean back against the counter, his eyes rolling in his skull toward heaven. "Of course I'm listening to you, Ophelia." He knelt to pick a styrofoam package of eggs from the bag on the ground. He walked over to the refrigerator, opened it and started placing the eggs in the egg bin, turning them so the bottoms rested at the base.

He listened to the chatter from the other side.

Eggs away, he let the door to the refrigerator shut and he pulled out a can of red beans, a package of rice. These he set aside and, remembering, turned to walk back to the refrigerator, which he opened to withdraw one of the bundles of celery from the crisper. *Close crisper. Close refrigerator. Place celery next to beans and rice. End this fucking conversation.*

"Ophelia, hey, yes, I gotta butt in here, I'm outraged too, and you're right, they're not doing enough and you're right there has to be someone we can write to clear up this situation, but you know what? Ophelia? Right now I'm dog tired. I didn't get any sleep last night—"

Chatter barrage. Eye-rolling.

"No, not because of Arturo. Christ, is that all you girls think about is sex? No. No sex. Nice. We had fun, it was fine. . . . No, I don't know if I'll see him again, well, I mean, yeah, of course I'll see him again, there's the gym and all, but as far as 'seeing' him, that I don't know, that I'm not so sure about. . . . Because, sometimes you don't know because. Because sometimes you really, really should just be friends with someone, and sleeping with them, sex, is just not a part of the program. . . . No, it's not because it's 'too early.' It's not too early." He scuffed his foot, his sock, along the tiling of the floor. "It's way late. Late. . . . Yes, actually, I do think Matthew would have been having sex by now with someone if the situation were reversed, but, it's not. It's not reversed and this is me and this is my life and God! why do I feel like you are becoming some bizarre kind of den mother for my whole existence?"

Chatter.

"Yes, and I love you for it too. Now, if you'll excuse me, I really do have to go make supper, and collapse these old bones of mine into bed before. . . . Red beans and rice, why? . . . Yes, your recipe Ophelia. . . .

"What about Elizabeth?" Adam rubbed his eyes, scratched his left leg with his right stockinged foot. "Yes, right, the proofs, yes, right, I forgot. Tell you what: have her leave them in front of my door, okay, on the landing? That'll be fine. There's room to do that and they'll be safe there and I'll get them. Tell her I'm sorry I can't see her and I'll talk to her about Matthew's book to-morrow but right now I have got to sleep." His legs shifted against the brown paper of the bag behind them. He smiled, weary, tired. "I love you too, Oph'. Thanks for caring. I know I don't say it enough. . . . G'night."

He hung up the phone. He took a bottle of Evian from the refrigerator, opened it, drank, and set it on the counter. He set the red beans to simmering in one pan, he boiled the rice in a small pot, and he washed and chopped two stalks of the celery, which he folded into the beans. He seasoned them with Old Bay, chili powder, garlic and basil. The rest of the celery he returned to the bin; he folded paper bags and tucked them away below the sink. He drank down another mouthful of water. He turned off the fire beneath the beans, beneath the rice. He drained the rice, spooned it out onto a plate, then poured the beans atop it.

He grabbed a fork from an open drawer which he closed with a bump of his hip. He tore off a paper towel and scooped his fist around the water bottle. He lugged all of this off to the bed-room, a flick of his elbow shutting off the kitchen light in pass-ing. He set the food, the water, down upon a nightstand next to the bed, scooting the clock out of the way.

He undressed. He ate supper. He left the dishes and the bottle on the floor by his bed. He turned out the light and went to sleep.

FINGERS FEELING THEIR WAY around the molding of win-dows, tapping out a silent rhythm to vibrate along the panes of the glass. His hand pressed itself flat against the pane of glass, he brought his face close to the glass; his breath warmed his hand and fogged the glass. He noticed the dirt beneath his fingernails, dirt from the flower boxes on the railing, dirt his fingers had sunk into as he grasped and pulled to quickly clamber aboard the porch. He pressed, harder, and his hand pushed through the glass, which landed with a shattering upon the hardwood floor within. He was pleased to note there was little blood on his part; the pane had fallen almost whole from the old molding. His wrist protected by the sleeve of his coat, he reached, grasped, and twisted the handle of the French door; he pulled, and the house opened to him.

Gingerly, he withdrew his hand from the empty framing and let his feet step quietly inside.

He listened. At first there was silence; then there was the hum of a refrigerator, to his right and behind that partition, he guessed. There was the sound of a clock ticking, also to his right but this was closer and yes, there it was, upon a table. Before him there was a couch, a small glass living room table. To his left there were bookcases, with picture frames upon them. He moved over to the bookcases, ran his fingers across their surfaces, leaving clean trails in the dust of the shelves; light greasy "X's" atop the glass of the pictures.

He moved toward the kitchen and a floorboard creaked under his foot.

He froze.

He waited.

Refrigerator.

Clock.

Silence.

He stepped lightly to what he had guessed was the kitchen and wasn't surprised to find himself correct. He stood on its threshold, he looked around it: small, clean, with empty countertops, washed dishes and a small table against the wall to his right; just before it, higher on the wall, a telephone. He reached out and with his fingertips deftly manipulated the plastic clip of the cord free from the body of the phone.

He turned left and stared down a hallway. He began to move down it slowly, his mind thinking, his body listening for every possible sound to be the beginning of another loose floorboard, or the sound of another's footsteps.

Refrigerator.

Clock.

Silence.

A door on his left; open it and see: a coat closet, home as well to mops and brooms. He shut it, with a small click.

Further down the hallway.

A door dead ahead. Another door to his left, and across from it, a door to his right. Which one first? Left: a den, a study, filled with bookshelves crammed with books, in the center of the room a large, heavy desk with a banker's lamp, a computer, beside the desk a printer; a chair. Behind all of this a window and before that, a window seat upon which lay a cushion, more books, loose pages.

This door too he shut with a small click. *Door number three, on the right?*

A bathroom. Shower, tub, toilet, toilet paper, soap, shampoo, magazines.

Again, the door shut with a small click. He stood at the end of the hallway, one door left before him. His hand reached down, felt the cold crystal of the knob. He took a deep breath, he steadied himself, he felt the pounding of his heart begin to quicken, he felt an excitement rise about him and spread itself throughout every fiber of his being.

He turned the knob. He opened the door.

He smiled.

He smiled.

Moonlight washed in from a rear window, spilling itself across a bed swathed in white sheeting against the far wall to his left. To his right, a dresser, atop which sat change, a photograph in a metal frame, a wooden bowl holding cuff links and small hoop earrings and a black pearl stud which he picked up, fingered to feel its smoothness, and held up to the moonlight to watch the color of blue. A chair, light, insubstantial to his immediate left and against the far wall, to his left of the window, another book-case filled to overflowing and to the window's left but hollowed out of his right wall, a door leading to (he guessed and knew, as with the kitchen, that he was correct) a closet, stuffed with clothes and shoes and whatnot.

Michael's hand stole quietly toward the inner pocket of his long coat, where he kept the pipe.

Adam slept, his body curled like a resting fetus, one hand tucked under his head and his other hand clutched to his chest. The lines of his body beneath the top sheet rose and fell with the deep evenness of his breathing, and he rustled the sheeting now and again with small dreamings.

Michael moved toward him, his feet padding toward the bed, soft upon thick Oriental carpets covering the floor. There were seven steps from doorway to bedside; conveniently, Adam slept on the right hand side of the bed, the side nearest the door, the side nearest Michael.

Step one.

Step two.

Step three and Michael fought to calm his breathing, excited in his chest.

Step four.

Step five and Michael shifted the warmth of his fingers upon the cool rough metal of the lead.

Step six.

Step seven and Michael's foot knocked against the thick

plastic of a bottle which toppled, soaking water onto the carpet. Michael stepped to avoid the plastic and his foot came down upon something hard and porcelain and it snapped, it popped beneath his feet with the clattering of silver and there was movement upon the bed.

THE SOUND ENTERING his sleep like the report of a gun and he rolled over, he saw, in the first moving of his vision the shape of a man at his bedside and at first he thought *Matthew?* but then, knowing, and there was the moving, a dodging of pipe and Adam pitched himself upward, driving his shoulder into Michael's kidney, trying to lift the tall man up, away from the bed, trying to pin him to the wall.

No luck. Michael's body weight sank down upon him and there was a jab, the lead pipe sunk its way into Adam's belly, withdrew, slammed its way against Adam's ribs on his left-hand side, slammed down upon his left clavicle and Adam pushed, Adam fought against a breaking of bone but he was pinned, trapped, Michael's knees now upon his chest and Adam closed his eyes, Adam thought about breathing and in his mind he saw it all, all the boxing, all the training, all the fighting; all the nights, the streets, two gutted corpses the first night out, Sanchez's unconscious form last night, the boy in the green T-shirt he had saved and Adam looked back and he saw more, he saw further he saw Matthew, he saw Matthew pinned against the wall, he saw Michael thwacking Matthew across the face with the lead pipe—*that lead pipe!*—and he saw Matthew lying there, propped against trash cans, the last moment Adam had to remember seeing Matthew alive, that moment before Michael's kick propelled him out into the street and Adam remembered the hospital, the body, seeing Matthew's body and what had happened to it, what Michael had done to this man, this person that Adam loved and Adam felt again, felt most of all wiping out all else, that tingling latent, building within his body since

Michael's beating, Adam felt the tingling wash over him, rise out of him and all was white before his eyes, all was white and this was death, he was dying but no, this was life and there was a pressure upon his chest and there was a fire within his heart and there was his body moving, responding. He moved, he rose up off the bed and his right arm reached out, his right hand gripped Michael's left wrist and there was the sound of small bones shattering.

Michael roared back, his hand dropping the lead pipe to clutch his broken arm. Adam leapt off the bed and darted for the living room, his body halfway down the hallway when there was a whirling behind him and he was tackled, flying with Michael's body weight pushing him, landing hard upon the wood floor of the living room and Michael was screaming, was yelling, grabbing the hair on Adam's head and slamming Adam face-first into the hardwood floor once, twice, again and Adam twisted, Adam moved and his elbow caught Michael in the throat and a small choking noise lurched from Michael's mouth and he let go of Adam's head and Adam spun about, Adam bucked Michael from him like a thirteen-year-old first-time rider at the rodeo and he moved, he scooted out from under Michael and as he did so his right knee came up and caught Michael square in the crotch and Michael cried out and doubled over.

Adam stood, his breath coming in ragged heaves, blood dribbling from his nose and lip. He swallowed; blood. He swallowed again. His tongue felt thick in his mouth. "I want," he said, "I want to know why."

Michael was using the wall and his good arm, his right one, to pull himself to his feet. He laughed at Adam's request; he laughed at the blood smearing his own face. "Why?"

"Why."

He leaned back against the wall, holding his crippled arm. His breathing was unsteady; rough. Adam saw Michael's eyes clear with revulsion and hatred, and the tall man spit out two words: "Why not?"

Adam shook his head. "Oh, man," he said, and his body began trembling. He shook his head again, his fists clenching and unclenching at his sides. "Oh, man," he said again, "that's it? That's nothing. That's—" Adam started losing it, Adam started falling apart, Adam started crying.

Michael smiled. "That's me."

Michael charged.

His shoulder caught Adam in the chest and they fell, they raced back toward the door, slamming against it then Michael was off Adam, Michael pulled back and once! Michael hit Adam in the face twice! Michael hit Adam in the face three times! Michael hit Adam in the face before decking him, back-fisting him and then Michael stepped back.

His hands were covered with blood but most of it was not his own. His wrist was broken.

Adam staggered a step away from the door. Michael backed up. Adam staggered out another step. Michael backed up once more, and once more, that smile crossed Michael's face. His tongue flicked out, licking his blood from his lips, tasting the ripe fullness. He took two steps back; he reared up he kicked, a kick that caught Adam square in the chest and sent him crashing through the wood of the front door.

"Adam!"

Adam's head snapped to his left, where he saw Elizabeth, frozen on the stairs. "Elizabeth! Call Clarence Smalling!"

Elizabeth saw Adam, saw the splintered door, saw blood. "But Adam—"

"Elizabeth! Go!"

Her hands fluttered about the package she carried. "But what about the manuscript?"

159

"Take it with you!" he screamed at her and she shrank back. Then, from inside:

"Company?"

Adam looked before him into the apartment, then over to Elizabeth. "Elizabeth," he bellowed, "for God's sake, go!" and he hurled himself back into the apartment. She heard the thud of his body landing against something heavy, she heard footsteps, movement, scuffling, and then she heard nothing more, for she was outside, and fleeing for a pay phone.

ADAM'S FIST CLIPPED Michael on the chin, snapping his head to the right. Adam swung again; Michael's head snapped left. Right-left, right-left. Adam drove his fist deep into Michael's left kidney, right kidney, Michael's gut, Adam's fists sore from the fleshy hardness of Michael's body. Michael doubled over and Adam brought his elbow down hard upon the nape of Michael's neck, sending him crashing to the ground.

Adam stepped clear. *Phone-phone. Kitchen. Phone! Call Smalling.* He turned away from the living room, headed for the kitchen. He stood in the entranceway. He reached for the phone, he started dialing, he listened to the phone: nothing. *What?* He checked the receiver, the cord: *The cord!* He had the plastic clip at the opening when Michael's left arm reached around Adam's throat to draw him back, pinning him against the muscular expanse of Michael's chest, and Michael's right snaked out to grab Adam's arm, twisting it behind him so that a whimper escaped his lips. Michael pulled Adam away from the kitchen, away from the telephone, propelling him into the darkness of the corridor, toward the bedroom, toward the pipe.

Adam felt the rough edges of Michael's breathing whisper about his ear. He felt the floor brush by under his feet. He felt tired. He felt beaten. Every bone in his body ached; his face hurt. This pain: he hadn't felt this way since the beating.

The beating. *This beating.*

Michael pitched Adam forward into the bedroom; Michael knelt and scooped up the lead pipe in his good arm, his right arm. He swung it loosely in his hand, remembering the heft of it. Adam watched him from the bed; Adam watched the pipe.

"If you just sit there, I'll make sure you die quickly."

Adam nodded.

"Close your eyes," Michael said.

Adam did.

Michael's hand drew the pipe up to trace tenderly down the lines of Adam's cheeks, along the lines of his jaw, back about the contours of his nose, his eyes. "Your eyes," Michael said, and the pipe whispered away from Adam's face as Michael drew it back.

Michael swung.

Adam ducked. He dipped low and rolled, knocking Michael off balance and swinging himself onto the floor, but Michael was up, Michael was on him, atop him again and this time there was the pipe. Adam jerked his head left, and heard the pipe hit carpet over wood; right, and the same. Adam's arms were splayed out to his side, the fingers of his hands fumbled for something, anything; his right hand grasped tufts of empty carpet, and Michael lay his weight upon it to pin him. Adam's left hand splayed out beneath the bed, fingers searching; Michael reared back slightly, pipe swinging behind him, bringing it forward Adam's fingers closed about something and he brought it out from under the bed he brought it up, fast, he shoved, it stuck, there was blood, something like thick water; Michael's cry and Michael was off him, Adam was free. He rolled away, Adam scrambled atop the bed and when he turned, when he turned to look he saw Michael clawing at his face with his right hand, the shaft of Adam's supper fork protruding from Michael's right eye. A scrambling of Michael's fingers and blood; the fork fell to the carpet. Safe upon the bed, Adam tried to wipe himself clear of blood and fluid with his hands.

Michael's fists pressed upon his face. He staggered back, toward the door.

Adam spoke the name he had heard Jimmy whisper last night. "Michael, stop."

Michael crept away from the voice, away from the doorway, into the hallway.

"Michael, stop."

Michael unfolded his hands over his face and a sound commenced from him like sobbing.

They were in the living room, surrounded by shards of front door; walls and floors streaked with blood. In the distance there were the sounds of sirens. Adam listened. They grew louder.

Michael was still backing away. Adam's shoulders sagged. He listened for the distance of the police cars, for the number of them, for the different wailing of an ambulance. Michael stood ten feet apart from him now; he was inching further back toward the door, toward the debris.

"Michael, please: stop." Adam stepped forward; Adam reached out. He touched Michael, gently, almost tenderly, on the arm.

Michael acquiesced.

EPILOGUE

Almost a month later, Adam stood on the sun porch and looked down into his wineglass, where he swirled around the last swallow of iced tea among a few chips of ice. He lifted the glass to his lips, he drank down the tea. It was sweet, almost fruit-flavored—the kind of tea served to you at wholesome restaurants where most of the clientele wear Birkenstocks and the table conversation runs the gamut from saving whales to saving the rain forest.

Ophelia snuck up behind him and wrapped her arms about his midsection, giving him a playful squeeze. Adam let out a groan and affectionately patted the hands clasped over his belly. He leaned back into her. "Hi," he said.

"Hi," she said, pressing her face against the back of his shirt. She rubbed her hands up and down over his abdomen. "When you gonna get a gut like most men your age?"

Adam leaned forward to set his wineglass down upon the ledge, between two planters. He leaned back again into his friend, his hands covering hers. "I'm gay, Ophelia, and all gay men know that flabby abdominals are the curse of the heterosexual middle class."

"Mm-hmm."

"What's that supposed to mean?"

"Means I think you're becoming a snob."

"Becoming?"

She squeezed suddenly, hard, and Adam wheezed as he tried to pull forward. He started laughing as he felt her hands separate to start tickling his sides. He tried to turn and fend her off but she wouldn't have it and they fell to the ground, rolling about there between wicker chairs and plant stands, until Adam was pinned, Ophelia atop him, her hands darting quick jabs of ticklish affection here and there, parrying any jabs of his own.

Their laughter carried through to the living room and Elizabeth stepped toward the doorway, her lips at the edge of a glass of red wine. Just before the French doors she stopped, and watched them a few moments from the shadows of the apartment. The wineglass lowered, she heard her lover laugh, Adam crying, "Uncle! Uncle! Un-cle!" and Ophelia's response of "Patriarchal pig!" and Adam yelling, "Aunt! Aunt!"

She turned and walked toward the shadows, the soles of her feet free of sandals and cool against the hardwood floors. She stepped over to the bookcase, her gaze traveling across the spines of books, some known, others unknown to her. Her stare flicked upward, to the photograph she took of Adam and Matthew once, it seemed, a long time ago; to the smaller photographs framed now and standing upright upon these shelves, their faces containing memory, bright and fading. She jumped at the low voice behind her.

"It'll never stop feeling terrible, you know. It'll just become something you live with, inside you, a part of you, in a way, weird, but kind of like all of the good stuff."

Adam. Elizabeth's mouth played with the rim of her wineglass again. She kept looking at a space between two photographs until she heard the sound of his feet padding away across the wood. She turned to see Ophelia sitting on the side of the couch; there was the sound of water running in the kitchen.

"You know, you could close the book on this. Save the rest of your grieving for when I die."

Elizabeth eyes widened at this and she blinked, suddenly, quite hard. She lowered the wineglass and shook her head. She mumbled, "I don't know how to do any of this."

"Any of what?" Ophelia's voice was smooth, comforting as good Scotch.

"Grieving. Being sad. Letting go." Her words now came in a rush. "You and Adam, you seem to have this thing managed: Matthew's dead and life goes on."

Ophelia: "Right."

"Well, it doesn't feel right to me." The wineglass raised again to her lips; she turned to face the bookshelves, the vacant spaces between photographs. "It hasn't felt right for a long time."

Ophelia's voice was close, next to her ear. Her lover's breath was warm upon her flesh. "This isn't your loss to covet or call, 'Lizbeth." She felt Ophelia's hands safe, squeezing her shoulders. "We follow Adam's lead here. It's his turn to call the play."

Elizabeth lowered the wineglass, her thumbnail pressing against its edge. She sniffled, then she laughed. Ophelia hugged her, her body fitting against Elizabeth's in a comfortable, reassuring natural way. Ophelia's voice was a whisper: "What's funny?"

"You." Elizabeth was smiling, though her eyes were wet and she sniffled now and again. "When did you start talking in sports metaphors?"

"I'm a dyke, dear." Ophelia kissed Elizabeth's shoulder through her shirt. "I'm the butch in this relationship, remember?"

"No," Elizabeth said, and she turned, her body still fitting against Ophelia's. Her arms went about her lover's as her head bent. There was the feeling of warm breath against a cheek and then Elizabeth kissed Ophelia, the kiss something warm and soft and strong and tender: tongues playing tag in the darkness of a cave.

"I don't think I'm old enough to watch this."

The women separated from the kiss. Elizabeth's hand slipped free of Ophelia's as Elizabeth walked across the wood to where Adam stood holding a full bottle of Chardonnay in one hand, three clean, empty glasses in the other. She stood in front of him, she looked at him; she smiled, she sniffled, she hugged him. Ophelia came up behind her quietly and took the wine and the glasses from Adam's hands and he hugged Elizabeth in return.

"Oh, Adam," was all Elizabeth said.

"SO, WHAT'D YOU DO with the ashes, anyway?" Ophelia poured the last of the Chardonnay into her wineglass and leaned forward to set the bottle down, upon the coffee table, next to the empty bottle of red and an earlier-drained, other bottle of Chardonnay. She slid off the arm of the sofa to sit beside Adam, who sat beside Elizabeth. All three now faced out the French doors, and they watched the sun set over the roofs of old buildings; chimneys, and rickety television antennas.

"Dumped 'em."

Elizabeth elbowed Adam in the ribs and tried to hide her laughter in her wineglass. Ophelia slapped his shoulder lightly.

Adam protested: "Well I did! I did, that's what I did: I dumped them." He settled down into the sofa. "Okay, okay." He toyed with his wineglass. He reached out and set it down upon the table before him. He picked up the empty bottle of red and drew it close to him. It rested snugly in his lap, and he began picking at its label. "You remember Puget Sound, that vacation Matthew and I took to the hotel in Eastsound, on Orcas Island? The place used to be some old rich guy's mansion and it was on this inlet, with a main house and then these two wings, these two big, sweeping wings—" Adam spread his arms out to either side, nearly dinging Ophelia's head with the wine bottle but she ducked "—one t'either side, opening, welcoming the water?"

The two women listened. Adam let his arms fall back into his lap and Ophelia relaxed.

"So I took them out there. I went out there and I rented a room, the room, the same room we had then. And I went for walks, or I sat by the water. I went everywhere we went, but everywhere I went I sprinkled some of his ashes, until they were all gone." He looked from Ophelia to Elizabeth, a tight smile upon his face. "Then I came home. Empty-handed." He looked to the wine bottle with its shredded label. "We were really happy there," he mumbled. "I think—I thought he'd like that, you know? Being someplace where we were really happy?"

Ophelia rubbed his arm. "I'm sure he would."

"Yeah." Elizabeth patted his leg.

They sat there for a while. They finished their drinks.

They thought about Matthew.

OPHELIA NESTLED HERSELF more comfortably against Elizabeth. "So now what?"

"Life goes on." Adam lay on the floor, his feet propped up on the armrest of the couch where the two women spooned. A breeze came through the French doors, slipping over them, dissipating into stillness. It was night; all the lights of the apartment were dark. The yellow light of the streetlamp was below them. Adam's eyes followed the pattern cut by white swaths of light through the cool darkness of the ceiling, the light moving across the room like a rapidly passing day; sunlight brought from the halogen fires of passing BMWs and Fords. He swallowed. He closed his eyes. He regulated his breathing to a count of five. "Life goes on," he murmured.

"And what about Mr. Sanchez?" Adam felt Elizabeth's foot nudge his.

"Friends," he said, emphatically. "Friends." He jiggled his feet restlessly against the armrest until Ophelia kicked him lightly and said, "Stop that."

"Anyway," he finished, "that's all I'm really ready for right now. For a while."

They listened to the sound of their own breathing for a time. Ophelia began humming "Jesus Loves Me," getting only as far as the first few lines before Adam reached out, snagged a pillow from the end of the couch and brought it up quickly to bop her softly in the face with it.

Ophelia took this as a full-on declaration of war and she twisted her body to roll off the couch and onto the floor, where the wrestling with Adam began anew; Elizabeth scurried, falling over the back of the sofa in her efforts to keep clear of the tangle. Adam was intent on revenge for this afternoon's ticklish episode; Ophelia was intent on retaining her title.

Elizabeth moved around them to pull the coffee table out of the way, the sound of her efforts muffled by the happy squeals of Ophelia and Adam's struggle. She stood there and watched the two, a bemused smile starting upon her face and by the time she was grinning, she had already yelled "Pocahontas!" and pitched herself into the fray, tangling her limbs with those of those she cared about, and Adam was yelling, "Two against one—that's not fair!" and Ophelia was yelling, "Get it girl!"

Later, in the night, when friends had gone and the house was silent, Adam would again walk out onto the sun porch. He would look out toward moonlight painting the roofs of old buildings; chimneys, and rickety television antennas with silver. He would bend low to smell the earth scent, the fresh, growing bouquet of the flowers in the flower boxes. He would stand there in the cool, still air. He would stand there and he would hug himself and he would think:

Matthew, I love you completely.

Happy at the thought, he would swing his arms out to his side and then across his chest, stretching. He would reach up, toward the stars, toward the moon, and he would reach for something ineffable, something even higher and, grasping it somehow he would bring it back to him with the wholeness, and with the thought:

I am back. It is over. I am back.

It is over.

"This is all far from over."

—Roman Straus
in *Dead Again*

ACKNOWLEDGMENTS

I am grateful for the financial assistance of my parents and Richard Day, Neal Eglash, George Hallameyer, Sandra Watt, and Margo Willits. Scott Pretorius, Mark Shaw, Peter Telep, Roland Thompson, and Terry Wolverton read the first draft and provided helpful suggestions. Matthew Carnicelli, Stacey Fleck, Jason Friedman, Steve Gere, Joni Hullinghorst, Paula E. Langguth, Robert Rodi, Mark Shaw (again), and Kim Stallwood helped fine-tune the work in its second and ultimately final form. Thanks to Derrick Buisch for the art. I am grateful beyond words to my friend and editor, Christopher Schelling, and his associate in publishing, Kera Bolonik.

Thanks to Guinness for the love.

A portion of the author's profits from this book will be donated to *Teaching Tolerance,* a publication of the Southern Poverty Law Center working to eradicate bigotry through education. For more information on *Teaching Tolerance,* please write to:

Editor
Teaching Tolerance
400 Washington Avenue
Montgomery, Alabama 36104

DUTTON

 PLUME

GREAT GAY FICTION

☐ **THE WEEKEND by Peter Cameron.** On a midsummer weekend, in a country house in upstate New York, three friends gather on the anniversary of the death of a man related to them all by blood or love. Their idyll is disturbed by the presence of two outsiders. "A tale of love, mourning, emotional risk-taking and off-center lives . . . it hovers in a corner of your memory for a long, long time."—Margaria Fichner, *Miami Herald* (274117—$9.95)

☐ **SAY UNCLE by Eric Shawn Quinn.** As a busy advertising executive and single gay man living in a conservative Southern town, Michael Reily doesn't exactly have parenthood on his things-to-do list. So when Michael discovers he's been named guardian of his infant nephew he finds he's taken on the most challenging job of his life. But he's determined to do it his way, with wit, resourcefulness, and spontaneity. (937803—$20.95)

☐ **LIVING UPSTAIRS by Joseph Hansen.** This novel is a poignant love story about lies, dangerous acquaintances, and the betrayal of innocence. When Hoyt Stubblefield ambles into the bookstore on Hollywood Boulevard where nineteen-year-old Nathan Reed works, his good looks and wry Texas charm hold the boy spellbound. Within a week, Nathan has packed his belongings and moves in with Hoyt. "Beautifully crafted, perceptive, and compassionate."— *Los Angeles Times Book Review* (269253—$9.95)

☐ **JACK OF HEARTS by Joseph Hansen.** The author brings Nathan Reed back for a second tender, funny, achingly truthful coming-of-age novel. The year is 1941, the place a small California foothill town. Nathan, at age 17 bewildered by sex, but sure he wants to be a writer, falls in among a little-theater crowd he hopes will stage his first play, and learns from them painful lessons in growing up. (939245—$19.95)

Prices slightly higher in Canada.

Visa and Mastercard holders can order Plume, Meridian, and Dutton books by calling
1-800-253-6476.
They are also available at your local bookstore. Allow 4-6 weeks for delivery.
This offer is subject to change without notice.

DUTTON

GAY FICTION

☐ **FATHER OF FRANKENSTEIN by Christopher Bram.** James Whale, the elegant director of such classic horror films as *Frankenstein* and *The Bride of Frankenstein,* was found at his Los Angeles mansion in 1957, dead of unnatural causes. Now the author explores the mystery of Whale's last days in this evocative and suspenseful work of fiction. "A wonderful novel . . . wickedly witty intelligence . . . Monstrously good."—Patrick McGrath

(93913X—$19.95)

☐ **GLAMOURPUSS by Christian McLaughlin.** Torrid, dishy, outrageously romantic, this hilarious novel is both a deliciously satiric skewering of the glitziest Hollywood has to offer, and a sweetly wicked boy-meets-boy tale of unrequited love. (938664—$19.95)

☐ **TRAITOR TO THE RACE by Darieck Scott.** Charged with the erotic power of the senses and the liberating power of the imagination, this novel introduces a bold new voice in American writing. This stunning debut explores homophobia and self-hatred in the black community through the story of a bi-racial couple's reaction to a brutal murder. It is a breakthrough feat of fiction even in a decade of vanishing taboos. (939121—$20.95)

Prices slightly higher in Canada.

GREAT SHORT FICTION

☐ **MEN ON MEN:** *Best New Gay Fiction* **edited and with an introduction by George Stambolian.** "Some of the best gay fiction, past, present and future . . . It's a treat to have it conveniently collected. And it's a treat to read. Hopefully the word will now spread about the riches of gay writing."—Martin Baumi Duberman (258820—$12.95)

☐ **MEN ON MEN 2:** *Best New Gay Fiction* **edited and with an introduction by George Stambolian.** "This collection includes some of the hotest (in other words, coolest) stories I've read anywhere. *Men On Men 2* is a rich late-eighties mix of love and death."—Brad Gooch, author of *Scary Kisses*.
(264022—$12.00)

☐ **MEN ON MEN 3:** *Best New Gay Fiction* **edited and with an introduction by George Stambolian.** This diverse, collection continues to explore the universal themes of fiction—love, family, and conflict—from the perspectives of such leading authors as Paul Monette, Philip Gambone, Robert Haule, Christopher Bram, and sixteen others. (265142—$11.95)

☐ **MEN ON MEN 4: Edited by George Stambolian.** As in past volumes, a powerful volume of literature that puts gay fiction the cutting edge of contemporary art, allowing us to experience some of the most dazzling, revelatory, and provocative prose in print today. (258567—$12.00)

☐ **MEN ON MEN 5:** *Best New Gay Fiction* **edited and with an introduction by David Bergman.** Again breaking fresh ground with both established and first-time authors of extraordinary talent, this fifth volume in the series addresses issues that are immediate and real—and dares to be naughty, sexy, and fun. This is not just remarkable gay fiction, but remarkable American writing.
(272440—$11.95)

Prices slightly higher in Canada.

Visa and Mastercard holders can order Plume, Meridian, and Dutton books by calling
1-800-253-6476.
They are also available at your local bookstore. Allow 4-6 weeks for delivery.
This offer is subject to change without notice.